# *Praise for Cory Idle and Back to the Hunt*

**"Exciting from beginning to end!"** —*Early Reader Review*

**"A thrilling read."** —*Early Reader Review*

**"Gripped me from the very beginning with authentic characters and engaging language."** —*Early Reader Review*

*"Back to the Hunt* was a quick read I couldn't put down. The character arcs were great, and the different hurdles that the main character had to overcome were well written. It was exciting from beginning to end. The difficulty of having to not only fight an enemy that they knew nothing about along with a surprising domestic enemy was incredibly thrilling." —*Early Reader Review*

*"Back to the Hunt* gripped me from the very beginning with authentic characters and engaging language. Cory Idle built the dynamics between the characters impeccably, capturing their complex relationships and bringing them to life. The way in which he built mystery and suspense around what was happening kept me desperate to read more. All in all, *Back to the Hunt* was a thrilling read, and I look forward to reading more from Cory Idle." —*Early Reader Review*

**"With government conspiracies that date by decades, spooky creatures, and a town with people who just won't do the right thing... Craig Eitel is the hero we all need."** —*Alex Williams, editor*

# *About the author Cory Idle*

Cory Idle, an author of fiction and lover of dogs, began his career in entertainment with a role in radio, running the news and sports department.

Preferring fiction, Cory started his writing career by utilizing his respect and knowledge of the US Armed Forces and his love of storytelling, instilled in him by his parents.

After readers positively received two short stories, Cory Idle began working on his debut novel, *Back to the Hunt*.

Idle enjoys camping, hiking, and traveling with family and friends when he's not writing. Cory is also a host on *Kiss The Reviews* on YouTube.

*Back to the Hunt* is a military sci-fi thriller, and Idle's debut novel.

Please follow @Cory_Idle on Twitter and @coryidle on Instagram!

# BACK TO THE HUNT

## A MILITARY SCI-FI THRILLER NOVEL

## CORY IDLE

**5310**
PUBLISHING

# BACK TO THE HUNT

## CORY IDLE

"Gripped me from the very beginning!"
—*Early Reader Review*

# 5310
## PUBLISHING

Published by
5310 Publishing Company

Go to 5310publishing.com for more great books!

SCAN ME

Our books may be purchased in bulk for promotional, educational, or business purposes. Please contact your local bookseller or 5310 Publishing at sales@5310publishing.com or refer to our website at 5310PUBLISHING.COM.

*BACK TO THE HUNT (1st Edition)* - ISBNs:
Hardcover: 9781990158902
Paperback: 9781990158926
Ebook / Kindle: 9781990158919

Author: Cory Idle
Editor: Alex Williams
Cover Design: Eric Williams

The first edition of *BACK TO THE HUNT* was released in March 2023.

ADULT FICTION
FICTION / Science Fiction / Military
FICTION / Thrillers / Military
FICTION / Thrillers / Suspense

Themes explored include: Speculative fiction; War, combat and military adventure fiction; Science fiction: apocalyptic and post-apocalyptic; Science fiction: military; Thriller and suspense fiction; Mythical creatures: Zombies and the undead; Iowa, United States

**Ex-soldier Craig is working as mall security after being discharged from the military... until he's called back. Now he needs to find and extract a dangerous bioweapon, save the townspeople from a rebel military uprising, and get out alive.**

*Acknowledgments*

*I would like to thank all the friends and family who allowed themselves to be thrown on the back burner while this story was being conceived. Your constant love, support, and patience made it possible to complete this process.*

*For Tiffany, you are truly my GPS.*
*Without you, I would be completely lost.*

OFFICIALS ONLY

COVERT

CLASSIFIED

SECRET OPERATIONS

DO NOT SHARE

SPECIAL OPS

NONPUBLIC

MILITARY PERSONNEL ONLY

REDACTED

TOP SECRET

DO NOT READ

UNDISCLOSED

MILITARY ONLY

BURN AFTER READING

BEHIND-THE-SCENES OPERATION

PERSONAL

FOR YOUR EYES ONLY

SECRET CONTENT

# ONE

**LIKE ANY OTHER CHILD WOULD** have been, and most adults for that matter, Ellen Montgomery was amazed by the sound of the massive plane flying so low to the ground. The eight-year-old girl had never taken in something so awe-inspiring. Her wonder quickly began to turn into abject terror as the three right engines of the six-engine military aircraft erupted into flames as it flew over her head.

"Ow, Mommy!" Ellen, Ellie to her parents, shouted as she clamped the palms of her hands over her ears, tears instantly streaming down her diminutive cheeks.

All she had cared about that morning had been showing off the prettiest of her pink dresses. More often than not, her mother would insist she wears her white dress to church on Sunday. But today, her mother bent to her daughter's will. At this moment, however, as her eardrums burst, she could have cared less about her clothing. The pain and confusion that had suddenly corrupted her idyllic Sunday afternoon led to Ellen throwing up that morning's breakfast. The waffles, completely covered in butter and drowned in syrup, had tasted like pure heaven going down. The sweet, buttery goodness, now mixed with ice cream and stomach bile, was covering her dress. Ellie collapsed to the ground, curled into the fetal position with her ears still covered, and relentlessly sobbed in pain.

Mrs. Montgomery desperately tried but could not help her daughter as she had to cover her own ears. Every fiber of her being told her that Ellie was the priority now. Whatever was happening, her daughter needed to be protected. She crawled, having fallen to the ground, the two feet to her daughter—a crawl that felt like two miles—and laid her body across Ellie's. The sound of the exploding engines would have been deafening if not for the fact that everyone's eardrums had burst from the original explosion, only three hundred feet above their head. The plummeting aircraft had Main Street of Helm's Hamlet, Iowa, imprisoned in a mix of chaos, terror, and insurmountable pain. A busy, perfect summer afternoon in the Midwestern United States had just turned into a horror show.

The flailing aluminum bird was descending faster and faster each moment, the piercing scream of the flame-engulfed engines getting louder and louder with each foot of altitude lost. Pieces of debris breaking off the aircraft had begun to pepper the citizens of the tiny, rural Iowa town, like mortar strikes from an unseen enemy combatant, killing whomever they landed on in a violent instant.

Finding the mythical strength a parent does in a life or death situation that involves their child, Mrs. Montgomery scooped up Ellie in her arms and began to sprint toward anything that looked like cover. The people screaming would have added to little Ellie's terror, but her obliterated eardrum spared her from at least one of the horrors today would bring.

Although the survivors were able to catch their breath, once cover had been found, they were far from safe. What felt like an earthquake, at least to people not used to actual earthquakes, gave way to the renewed screams from those not quite ready to meet their maker. Everyone that still had their hearing was treated to one last enormous explosion erupting through the air, blowing out the windows along the now body-strewn street in the Midwestern United States.

The terror they could not hear was visualized for anyone still on the street as a huge fireball rose over the horizon and rose skyward like a volcano had just erupted. The events of the last three to four minutes had completely devastated an entire rural community. Those who found shelter started to emerge from their hiding spots to assess the damage and look for answers. What they found was their neighbors, friends, and family dead in the street. Some had been crushed by the falling hunks of metal. Some were trampled to death when a few hundred of their contemporaries ran for their lives, unaware of the people they were stepping on.

The fireball, looking like it was just over a mile out of town on Tom Donaldson's farm, had given way to a massive black cloud of smoke. There was no more debris falling from the sky, and even some of the shouting and crying had dampened down to whimpers. Sirens typically used for tornado warnings began to ring out, indicating to people that they needed to seek shelter immediately, tune into the local AM radio station, and do not attempt to move unless there was a life-threatening emergency. Another set of sirens, these from the two Type 2 fire engines and the three ambulances the small town had to offer, fired up as the crews prepared themselves for combat triage—as opposed to the minor fender benders, toaster fires, or the kittens in a tree type of emergencies they had grown accustomed to. The decision had been made that the wounded on the street, their neighbors and friends and family, were more important than the burning airplane.

"Nobody could have survived that," the burly, mustachioed fire chief had said.

The sun had begun to set by the time the various first responders had triaged most of the patients from Main Street and had sent the high-risk cases to the hospital, followed by those with less than life-threatening injuries. The ten full-time and five volunteer first responders began to catch their breath when it was decided it was time to turn their attention to the rising black smoke two miles east of town.

"Bailey, I want to take truck one out to the crash site. If you find anything that *actually* requires our attention, radio back to us. My guess is we're letting that diesel fuel burn itself out, but we got to check it out. Take your team out there. I will stay here with Team Two," the Fire Chief said to his lieutenant.

Lieutenant Bailey nodded and loaded up with Tucker James, his driver/engineer, Ronnie Lawson and Ronnie's brother, Tony—his two best paramedics. They flipped their sirens back on and screamed away from Main Street, watching the sun fade below the horizon. As they got closer, they saw that they were not the first professionals on the scene. A stern-faced, clean-shaven man in camouflage fatigues stopped the truck by stepping into the road and holding his hand up, palm out—the universal sign for "stop."

"We have everything under control here, folks," the camouflaged man said.

"Do you, soldier?" asked Lt. Dan Bailey from the passenger seat.

The armed soldier squeezed his rifle a bit tighter, his posture more defensive, and squinted so hard at Lt. Bailey almost looked like he had closed his eyes.

"Move along," he said, his voice still monotone, but his words' intent was not missed.

"Move along or else," was what the soldier had really been saying.

The sixty-two-year-old, slightly overweight lieutenant in the Helm's Hamlet Fire Department was not in a position to ask, "Or else what?"

"I'm not trying to fuck with you, son," Bailey said.

The army lieutenant had turned away but was now moving toward the passenger side door where Lt. Bailey was seated.

"Step out of the vehicle, sir."

Lieutenant Bailey complied reluctantly and took his chance to explain himself.

"I'm only sayin' you've got no emergency vehicles out here. I can tell from here that nobody survived. We don't need the ambulances, but you need to get that fire out. We can help. It's what we do. Please, let us help you."

The army private, whose name patch read Dillon, opened his mouth to respond but stopped and looked over his right shoulder. They all had heard it. The sound that had captured Private Dillion's attention sounded like an animal screaming. No, not screaming, squealing. A happy, delightful squeal, like a literal pig in shit.

Private Dillon looked at Bailey, fear took over his face, and ordered, "Get the fuck out of here, now!"

"Go! Go! Go!" Bailey exclaimed, jumping back into the fire engine as quickly as he had ever moved. His desire to help had evaporated, and his fight-or-flight response told him that flight was the only option. Unclear as to what was happening, Tucker slammed the gas down. Still in drive and picking up some speed, the vehicle began to lurch forward. Bailey shouted for Tucker to stop as they headed straight for the plane crash site. It was too late.

The truck was surrounded by thick black smoke. The same squealing was heard just outside now as the truck was struck hard on the left. The truck was hit so hard that the left side tires rose off the ground momentarily, making the men brace themselves for the heavy red truck to turn over. Instead, it ungraciously fell back on its tires and was struck again, this time the sound of the truck's metal frame being shredded.

The black smoke made it impossible to see anything not in front of their face. They all put on their gas masks, the relief of the fresh oxygen hitting their lungs easing their breathing. The rotating but silent red siren at the top of the truck made an eerie red mist that fell and dissipated as it mixed with the thick smog. Initially, Bailey thought they were being pelted by heavy shrapnel from the burning aircraft. Then, a third hit on the side of the truck and Bailey started to change his mind. It felt as though someone, or something, intentionally was trying to knock them over.

"Tucker, if you ever want to see your wife and kids again, you need to get us the fuck out of here!" Bailey shouted.

Tucker shifted the vehicle into reverse and stepped on the gas. The heavy emergency vehicle jumped backward but hit something.

"Lieutenant?" Tucker questioned. The fear in his eyes could have been seen from space.

"Stay here. I'll check it out," Bailey said, a tremor in his voice.

Bailey exited the vehicle and made his way to the rear of the truck. The bumper was bent in the middle and there was a massive dent where the station's insignia had been painted on. He looked around, unable to see much more than a foot in front of him, and decided it was time to get the hell out of there.

"Reverse, back to the road, now!"

Tucker complied and backed out of the inferno, starting to laugh uneasily as people do after a near-death experience. Back on asphalt, the truck came to a stop next to Private Dillion and his armored vehicle. Dillion had his rifle fixed on Tucker.

"Exit the truck now!"

Tucker, no longer laughing, put the truck into park and threw the driver's side door open. Tucker was out of the vehicle with his hands raised when another loud squeal was heard from the fire. Dillion took his rifle from Tucker and pointed it toward the crashed aircraft. The sweat dripping from his brow had Tucker more scared than the sounds coming from the burning cornfield.

"Get out of here, now," Dillion whispered, his voice wrought with fear.

Tucker put his hands down and turned back around to get inside the truck. Before Bailey could tell him to hurry the hell up, Tucker James, aged twenty-seven, was snatched away and lost in the night's sky.

Bailey swore he saw a hand come out of the smoke but was too afraid to rationally think at this point. He sat there, frozen in his seat, arm outstretched, trying to grab a person who seemingly vanished into thin air. He had a wife and a young kid. He was real. They had been friends. But now he was just... gone.

*Had there been a hand? Davis didn't fly away... did he? No, he didn't. I saw a hand. No, two hands! Two big hands with long grotesque fingers,* Bailey thought to himself but still couldn't believe it. He wanted to shout out to his employee and friend but couldn't find his voice.

Throwing himself across the driver's side seat, Bailey reached to shut the driver's side door. He was desperately stretching out but too fat and old to grasp the handle. Not even coming close, Bailey took a deep breath, unbuckled his seat belt, and jolted himself fully out of the passenger seat. The tips of his middle finger could feel the cool steel of the metal door handrail, a feeling that was damn near euphoric against his skin.

That feeling vanished just as quickly as Tucker had when an ice-cold, clammy finger met his. He tried to recoil, but it was far too late. The same two hands he swore had snatched Tucker from him, now had a grip on Bailey's wrists. What he hadn't seen before was the flaky, white skin and long black fingernails. As they dug into his wrist, a face came into view. He desperately wanted to close his eyes but could not resist looking into the face of evil. It was slightly hidden by the thick smoke, but the grin and licking lips of the creature were plain as day. Bailey began to rattle off an incoherent prayer as he was fully plucked from the fire engine.

The two men sitting in the back of the cab did not move or make a sound... Even when it was their turn to be tasted.

# CLASSIFIED

## TWO

**THE GREENVILLE MALL HAD SEEN** better days. When he was a kid, growing up in this town afforded little in the way of entertainment, save for the mall. The kids who went to the same high school as he did would roam the single-floor shopping center, exploring the twenty or so various stores. "All under one roof," as the advertisements would exclaim. It was the ideal place for boyfriends to meet girlfriends and girlfriends to break up with boyfriends. Friends were made and rivals would fight in the parking lot. "The Mall" was the place to be... twenty years ago. Today, this once shining monument to the "capitalism in hyperdrive" of the eighties was a shell of its former self. Craig felt the same way, laughing at the fact that he was able to empathize with a dilapidated building more so than he could with a human being. They were both like a cicada's exoskeleton, clinging to a tree trunk, void of soul or purpose.

The stern-faced security guard looked at the nearly empty parking lot from his security vehicle. The early 2000s two-door sedan had seen better days—much like the mall, much like himself. Craig had held this position for three years, the guy before him another ten. As far as they both knew, the two-door, fuel-efficient car was already pretty well used at that time. The irony of a broken man sitting in a run-down car, guarding an irrelevant building, did not escape him.

Summer was coming to an end, Craig noted, as the sun seemed to be setting earlier and earlier each day. The only benefit, as far as he saw it, was at least the vehicle was smelling less and less like a fart-powered garbage dump after soaking all day in the midwestern summer sun. Just as he was about to start drawing philosophical conclusions using the approaching fall season as another metaphor for his own withering life, Craig heard the modified exhaust of the two-door hatchback remodeled into a street racing car. The one he had been waiting for.

Jimmy Spaski and his group of shithead friends had been terrorizing the citizens of Greenville, Ohio, for the last year. Until today he had never been made to pay for his crimes. Some folks thought it was because his father was Sheriff David Spaski, a corrupt man in his own right. Others figured that nobody wanted to testify against the little shit, but Craig knew the truth. He had known guys like Jimmy his whole life. Jimmy was able to skate through life because his nihilistic attitude made him almost impervious to shame. How do you punish someone that simply does not care? Was rehabilitation even possible for someone like Jimmy Spaski or was his fate inevitable?

Just last week, everyone knew Jimmy and his crew beat and robbed Mrs. Teague, the seventy-year-old, widowed woman that had worked at the Knits and Knacks store in the mall. She was, of course, interviewed by the sheriff, Sheriff "Daddy" Spaski, that is, and she decided that she could not identify any of her attackers. The rumor then, as was the case in most small towns these days, was a group of black guys or illegal immigrants were prowling the streets, ready to attack old women and your daughters. That little party of theirs was the reason Craig decided that today was the day. Was it his job? No, it was not. He had been a soldier once upon a time. A blunt instrument used to protect people. This was all he knew, no matter how hard he tried. For the last three years, he had been an unused hammer. Jimmy Spaski was the nail he had been waiting for.

Craig waited for the sound of Jimmy gassing his engine when parked. The kid did this every time he parked the car, one last show of misplaced dominance by the young punk. When he heard the engine rev angrily, Craig started his car. He knew Jimmy probably wouldn't care even if he had heard Craig's engine start, but him being thorough was something that had kept him alive in actual combat situations. It was a habit you did not break easily, if ever.

He paused for one minute and fifteen seconds, the approximate time it would take Jimmy and three of his cohorts to walk from his usual parking spot to the mall's entrance, before Craig began to slowly drive the car around to the other side of the mall and the parking lot on the south side of the property. He let the car coast through the empty lot until he was up next to Jimmy's car. Glancing around one last time, Craig got out of his car, now parked directly in front of Jimmy's vehicle. He calmly walked around to the rear of his vehicle and unlocked the trunk. Digging through the trash and various pieces of emergency equipment, Craig found the large knife he had been looking for. He set it on the rear bumper and began to once again rifle through the trunk, this time pulling a crowbar from beneath the stacks of papers and trash. Leaving the trunk open, he walked around to the driver's side front tire and stuck the long filet knife deep into the rubber. Pulling the knife out, the air started to violently hiss from the punctured tire. Once he had circled the car, puncturing all four tires, he tossed the knife back inside the open trunk and gripped the crowbar with both hands as he swung it into the front windshield. The glass cracked at the center of where he struck the windshield and splintered until it spread across the entirety of the glass. As he moved around to the back, he heard Jimmy call from behind him. Craig estimated Jimmy was just at the mall's entrance but approaching fast.

"What the fuck!"

Craig turned around and smiled his best shit-eating grin and waved with his right hand still holding the crowbar, "Oh, hey, fellas."

"You've gone too far this time, baldie," Jimmy said, running up to Craig.

Craig noticed the three guys with Jimmy had begun to surround him. He smiled a bit, appreciating the tactical awareness of the would-be gang... even though it wouldn't matter much in the end. Craig was about to start speaking when he felt the phone in his right pocket vibrating. He held up a finger to the confused and very pissed-off Jimmy, pulled the phone from his pocket, and checked the caller id. The phone screen read: "private number."

Craig hit the ignore button, put the phone back into his pocket, and opened his mouth to speak again. The phone started vibrating again. Frustrated, he took the phone from his pocket and saw that the caller ID read the same as before. Once more he decided to ignore it. He put the phone back into his pocket and apologized to the gang for the interruption.

"So, James, let me explain," Craig began, his hands up in the air innocently with the iron crowbar still in his right hand.

"You can explain it to the doctor, mother fucker," Jimmy snarled, so angry he sounded like he was about to cry.

Craig exhaled, pretending as if he didn't want this the whole time, "I'm not an old lady, James. Your words and actions over the past year alone demand justice. You all need to understand that all actions have consequences. *Your* actions have brought vengeance."

The man directly to his rear, Danny Green, was the biggest of the three guys, weighing in at two-hundred-fifty-some pounds. Thankfully for Craig, he was also the dumbest. Danny's heavy first step was all Craig needed as he planted his left foot steadfastly behind him and spun from his hip with his left elbow, raised ear high. The speed of the elbow combined with the momentum of the heavyset nineteen-year-old created a loud crack as they connected with one another. Craig saw Danny's eyes flutter but was not waiting to watch the big man fall down.

His second target, a skinny, dirty kid named Brandon, was still watching in awe as Danny fell to the ground with a thud. The poor bastard never saw the crowbar fly into the bridge of his nose. He was, however, able to see the blood spurt from his nose. Craig caught the crowbar with his right hand as it bounced off of Brandon's face. With a broken nose, he knew Brandon would be a nonfactor for the last few seconds left in this fight.

Craig made a quick, stuttering hop to his left and planted his left foot into the stomach of the third man, Scotty Jenkins. Scotty had done some minor jail time for small felonies but was as soft as baby shit. Of all the guys that ran with Jimmy, Craig had wished any of the other guys had been there today. Scotty was no angel, but he was hardly a threat, especially to someone with Craig's abilities. Sometimes though, you just get stuck in the wrong place at the wrong time. He hoped Scotty learned this lesson as he watched the kid gasp desperately for the air Craig had just stolen from him.

With his back turned, having just delivered the hard side kick to Scotty's stomach, Jimmy bit his lip and took his shot. With everything he had, he buried his fist deep into Craig's kidney. Craig arched back, more out of surprise than in pain, and he felt Jimmy's foot on the back of his knee. Having turned his back on Jimmy was a mistake, but thanks to this kid's lack of any real experience, Craig was not as vulnerable as he looked.

He fell to the ground, tucked himself into a ball, and propelled himself forward. Rolling into the unconscious body of Scotty, Craig used it as a bumper to propel himself back onto his feet. He was now facing forward and saw Jimmy reaching into the back of his jeans. Thinking it was a gun, Craig quickly picked up some of the loose gravel on the ground of the parking lot and threw it into Jimmy's eyes. Giving him no time to think, Craig lunged at Jimmy, tackling him to the ground, rolling over the top of him like a summersault, and tossed Jimmy into the passenger door of the security vehicle. Jimmy hit the ground with a thud and did not move for a few seconds. Craig was worried he had killed the little fuck but breathed a sigh of relief when he saw the snot bubbles in Jimmy's nostrils moving in and out in a rhythmic motion.

The sound of the police sirens was almost enough to distract Craig from the vibrating phone in his pocket. Craig, annoyed, took the phone from his pocket and saw the caller ID now read: "General Maxwell Andrews." In a flash, the part of his life he thought was over came flooding back to him. He wanted nothing to do with whatever this was. He had given a part of his hip, two pints of blood, his conscience, his pride and hope for this country. What else could they possibly want from him?

Craig Eitel, formerly known as Staff Sergeant Eitel, USMC, had retired. To be more accurate, he had been retired. An exemplary soldier during his time in uniform, he could have won every award a military man could win, assuming any of the operations he had been involved in had been "on the books." As is so often the case, the men and women who really changed the course of history, the ones who actually won wars, are often lost to it.

Nothing more than a footnote in an otherwise apathetic universe. Sure, people wore ribbons and flew flags, attended parades, and ate hot dogs on the fourth of July... but none of them actually cared. Everyone in uniform knew it, even if they couldn't admit it.

As a younger man, like all young men, he was idealistic. Craig was the moron that saw the marine on TV, slaying dragons with a sword, and wanted to do nothing else. All he had ever wanted to do was slay dragons. Whether it was the literal dragon from his fairy tales as a kid, a bully in elementary school, or the head of a terrorist organization—he wanted to smite them all. While no man is born a saint, salesman, or shithead, many inside the Department of Defense, and all of its many branches, regarded Craig as the closest thing to a natural-born soldier.

What none of his experiences had taught him, however, was how to deal with the inevitable loss of brothers. Fighting next to someone else forms a brotherhood. You can call it a cliché if you wish, but it proves itself true time and time again. The bond two people form when fighting next to each other, literally saving each other's life with every round fired. Taking another life to save the guy next to you. That man doing the same for you. In those moments, all the God, flag, and country rhetoric flies out the window. All you are fighting for is the safety of your unit. The rest are semantics and completely irrelevant.

The horror of failing those brothers, the failure of not bringing them home, is enough to keep the average Joe up at night. A lot of professional badasses still can't sleep without reliving their worst moment over and over again. The one time you have a bad day at work. That one day you have a case of the Mondays. People die. Friends. Men and women with families. Families you have to face. Faces looking you square in the eyes, knowing your failure is the reason for their eternal grief. While Craig thought about them often enough, it was the living men he wished he could be with.

With a sigh, Craig resigned himself to two truths. One, if he answered that phone, he would relive it all again. Dead brothers lying all around him. Men that survive, hung out to dry by the very country they were protecting. To answer that phone was like escaping hell and asking to go right back.

Craig's second truth, in this tragically brief moment of clarity? He knew there was no way in hell that phone call was going to voicemail.

# THREE

**"IKE," A VOICE FROM HIS** past started, "It's General Andrews. I've got Vernon Smith from the agency with me. Not to mention a whole other heap of folks from agencies I've never even heard of. We're gonna need ya to come in, son."

His voice, while turning to gravel with age, still had the Texas twang that Craig had always found humorous.

"Yeah, General. I'm going to stop you there. I'm about to be arrested on assault charges against four persons and my company vehicle. Whatever it is you're calling about, you may have to wait three to six months—possibly two with good behavior."

"Jesus, Ike. Some things never change, do they?" the general had asked rhetorically and with a chuckle.

General Andrews put his hand over the receiver, but Craig could still hear him yelling for Smith to contact the Darke County Sheriff's Department.

"Don't worry about the fuzz, son. We'll take care of that. We've had a bit of a situation here... and well, I've been authorized to bring in the best we got. No pussy footin' around this time."

"Can you give me any details now," Craig replied solemnly.

"Negative, Ike. We—" Andrews had begun but was cut off, something the general was not accustomed to.

"Craig, it's Smith. Get to Greenville Airfield. We have an aircraft waiting for you. We'll brief you in person."

"Are the cops going to be chasing me there?"

"Negative. Just get in your car and get to the airfield."

The general jumped in the conversation again. Clearly a bit pissed he was interrupted. "Craig, this is a big one. Shit, this may be *the* big one. We need you, son."

With that, the line disconnected from Craig's end. Andrew's eyes shot furiously at the CIA man. Andrews, maybe thirty years senior, was ready to teach this kid a lesson. A career man, a member of the Joint Chiefs of Staff, did not rise to the occasion every time a little brat wanted to flex his muscles, but every rule had an exception.

"Do you have a problem, Vern?"

"You and your little bromance with this asset is disturbing to me. You have no idea..."

Now it was his turn to interrupt, "No, son, you have no idea. I get that you bunch of paper-pushing jerk-offs got together with a bunch of scientists and may have completely fucked the people of Iowa, the United States, and possibly the world. I am a four-star general in the United States Marine Corps, a member of the Joint Chiefs of Staff, and was fighting in actual wars when you were playing war on your little pussy video games. Do not ever presume anything about me, let alone my divulging of classified material over a Goddamn cellular network. If you have any more concerns, write them down on some paper and save them for your next shit. Are we clear?"

"You're right, General Andrews. I apologize. This is just... bad. I mean, I know we've been to the brink before, but this feels different. I don't see any way around it. This could be uncontainable. I'd just presume we put the hammer down on the whole damn area."

General Andrews took a breath and paused another second, considering Smith's concerns. Feeling enough time had passed to seem sincere, Andrews took Smith by his shoulders, looked him in his eyes, and hoped he was telling the truth.

"With Craig on this, we can control it. With the right team, we *can* control it. We're carpenters. He's the hammer. Let the tool do the work before we decide the house should be condemned."

The agent exhaled directly into Andrews' face, and the smell of his egg salad sandwich lunch was now invading every pore the general had. Disgusted, he pulled away.

"For God's sake, Smith. When we're working this closely together, you can carry a toothbrush and toothpaste, chew gum or not eat. The choice is yours, but you will make it before we do anything else."

Sheepishly, Smith turned away from the general and mumbled, "Yes, sir," before setting off in search of fresh breath.

# OFFICIALS ONLY

## FOUR

**A VERY LONG AND UNEXPECTEDLY** turbulent two-hour flight brought Craig to a small airfield just outside of Helm's Hamlet, Iowa. The six-seat, twin-engine private plane that the government had sent would have been considered a luxury most days. Unfortunately, it felt more like a hearse to Craig. Once he had gotten off the aircraft, he got into the backseat of a blacked-out four-wheel drive SUV without saying a word to anyone or anyone saying a word to him.

Craig stared out the window wondering how he had been dragged back into the freak show. He had made it out. A retired man from his profession was usually considered a win in anyone's book. Death was an expected part of the job. Everyone that wore the uniform understood that. Understanding something in theory, however, is a far cry from actually facing the reality of no longer existing. He had made it out, but now he was back. Drawn in by a simple phone call. At that moment, Craig was very disappointed in himself.

*Why would you keep doing this to yourself? What could possibly be so horrible that he would willingly pick up another rifle and go to work?*

Even if the questions had not been silent and rhetorical, Craig felt the need to answer himself.

*Because you're an addict, you moron. You're a junkie. No different than those sad bastards getting injected with naloxone when they overdose. The only difference is that you're not addicted to smack, pills, heroin, or any other narcotic. You are addicted to something far worse. You are addicted to your job... no. Be honest. You are addicted to the hunt, and there was no greater challenge for a hunter than hunting another man.*

The vehicle jerked to a stop, snapping Craig out of his head. The large depot, typically used as a maintenance and weather facility during the icy Iowa winters for highway maintenance staff, had been completely transformed. The forward operating base was impressive, even to a guy who had seen damn near everything. The number of uniformed men and women running around would have looked like chaos to an outsider. Hell, it damn near looked that way to Craig, save for the fact that he had lived in the eye of the storm for most of his adult life. Each pair of boots stomping around in a hurried mess held a determination as they worked like a well-choreographed ballet. Craig, based on the fact he was there, witnessing firsthand the manpower and effort being lent to this operation, knew this was no mom-and-pop op. Something serious was happening in the heartland of America.

Before his mind could wander too far, Craig saw two men emerge from the crowd. Like Moses parting the Red Sea, the general walked forward as the crowd split right down the middle. Nobody stopped to salute the man. They simply removed themselves from his path, yet another indication that something big was happening. Craig had worked with General Andrews on a few operations over the years. As Craig was called on more and more to eliminate targets around the world, the general would often be his military liaison or point person. The two had formed a bond over the course of each mission. Every time Craig did his job, especially with no military casualties, the general would earn more of those precious gold stars on his shoulder, which continued to elevate his position. Every time General Andrews had worked with Craig, the missions were thorough, well-executed, and never required the use of a backup plan. Well, mostly every time.

The other man walking alongside General Andrews, Craig assumed, was the agency man.

*What did Andrews say his name was*, he asked himself.

Before Craig could come up with the answer, the slender man with two-day-old beard stubble and a coffee-stained, white button-down shirt with the sleeves sloppily rolled up had thrust his hand out aggressively.

"Agent Smith. Vernon Smith, damn glad to have you on board," he said smiling.

He was shaking Craig's hand for an uncomfortable amount of time but became transfixed by the man's yellowed front teeth. Craig guessed this guy smoked about two packs and drank half a bag of coffee a day.

*God forbid the agency only had single-serve coffee machines. Those things would become sentient just to beg for mercy from this would-be coffee pod sadist*, he thought to himself with a subdued chuckle.

Craig just smiled and returned the vigorous handshake in an attempt to stop holding the agent's hand any longer.

The general, watching just as dismayed as Craig, cleared his throat and said, "Yes, we're all very excited to have you back on the team."

Smith snapped back to reality and, with his arm extended toward the internal workings of the base, showed Craig which way he could begin to walk. General Andrews walked with him on his left while Smith jumped to the front of the caravan, leading the way to a small round table.

Four men in black polo shirts, tucked into nondescript khakis and military-issued boots, had begun to sit down, with what smelled like strong fresh coffee, as Craig and his escorts approached. The well-built, hard-faced men looked at Craig in his cheap white button-down shirt, navy-blue slacks, and the patch just above his heart that read: "Greenville Mall Security." A few of them scoffed while one of the guys at the table rolled his eyes. Craig did not blame them, he forgot that he was in his work uniform.

"General, can you get me some fatigues? I look like an asshole."

The general smiled and got an assistant's attention with a hand gesture. He whispered into the young soldier's ear and sent him off in a hurry.

"We'll get you fixed up," General Andrews said.

"Craig, this is the team we have assembled. They'll be your escorts on this little excursion," Smith said with the proud smile of a father.

Craig nodded in their direction, and the team returned the silent greeting.

"We'll have time for names and hobbies a bit later," Andrews piped in. "For now, let's get down to business, gentlemen."

A couple of the guys snickered at the way Smith's voice dropped an octave when he addressed the team, but for the most part, everyone around the table was already in business mode. Craig liked to see that. Too loose of a group often meant mistakes. Mistakes got people killed. Craig would not tolerate mistakes.

A large white screen suspended from the ceiling was lit up by the start of a large projector. The illuminated screen had "Project Brains" and "Classified" in plain block lettering shown on the first page of what was the start of a presentation on the mission.

"What we have here is classified at the highest levels. Any mention of this project even existing outside of the mission parameters and you'll be rat fucked off to Gitmo," Smith said then paused for a moment, looking at everyone's face before he continued.

Craig rolled his eyes. Everyone at this table was a professional. Telling this group that divulging classified material was just cause for sending them to Guantanamo Bay with no trial or due process was like telling a baseball player to try to hit the ball with the bat. Smith's general disposition and his ridiculous bravado made the decision easy. If anything went wrong during this operation, Craig knew exactly who he would blame it on.

Satisfied his warning had been heard, Agent Smith clicked the small remote control in his hand, and a new slide appeared on the screen. The next five or six slides all looked the same to Craig. The slides were full of chemical and math equations he did not comprehend, and he only recognized a few words like "population destabilizer," "biological weapon," and "nonlethal fungal bacteria."

Smith, seeing he was losing his audience, began using layman's terms to brief the team.

"Basically, the United States began to develop nonlethal ways of destabilizing a city population after we were run out of Saigon. These ranged from the ridiculous, like mind control projects through military R&D, to the more feasible, like testing chemical agents that were nonlethal. After the Cold War, and with little to no success, the funds were allocated to other projects, and everything was shut down. After 9/11, Congress very quietly reallocated those funds back to us. The agency, along with numerous other private think tanks and laboratories, started to stretch our wings and really shoot for the stars. Fortunately, nature gave us one hell of a good start. We were made aware that the US government was in possession of something that was game-changing. Are we all good so far?"

"No," Craig said. "We are not good so far. Can you tell us what you found?"

"Tell me, do any of you know anything about zombie ants or cordyceps?"

Nobody raised a hand, so Smith continued, "Cordyceps is a natural fungus in nature. Without going into a deep dive as there are over four hundred types of this fungi. We will be focusing on one, *Ophiocordyceps unilateralis*, otherwise known as the Zombie Fungus.

A hand rose up slowly from the group. A tall, thick-necked man stood after Agent Smith recognized him. "Sir, did you just say zombies?"

Smith replied, "Yes, but not like you think. First, a bite is just a bite. It is no more spread through a bite than cancer is. This is an airborne fungal bacterium."

"Airborne? How far can it spread before it becomes ineffective?" Craig asked.

"One 'spore bomb,' as we call them, can spread up to five miles. Upon arrival, the spores become activated and can survive for seven hours without a host. The results are... lasting."

"Define lasting," Craig demanded.

"Permanent," Smith replied solemnly.

One of the other men at the table, a short Latino guy with a thin beard, asked, "So if they don't bite, what do your zombies do?"

"The fungus, in nature, can control the host's central nervous system. It forces the ant to go to a specific place at a specific time and essentially wait to be eaten. Antennas, controlled by the fungus, grow out of the ant's head which signals to predators that a meal is ready."

"This is all great, but the man asked you what your zombies do," Craig reminded Agent Smith.

The agent looked around the room, a bit embarrassed, before continuing, "The cordyceps that we know of do not have any adverse effects on human beings. A mining expedition, some time ago, found a spore that could impact human beings. My zombies, as you insist on putting it, behave recklessly. Like the ants, an infected subject will grow antennas and behave counterintuitively to their survival. They basically kill themselves, any way they can."

Smith had been working the projector with a remote and paused now on a picture of an infected human subject. The antennae, as he called them, looked like long, skinny mushrooms growing out of the patient's frontal bone. Their eyes were white as if the subject had cataracts. If he was pausing on this picture for dramatic effect, Craig thought, it worked. The silent table just looked at the picture in horror. Understanding he had their complete attention now, Smith continued.

"Less than eight hours ago, a cargo plane departed a laboratory in Nevada, carrying the last of the cordyceps. They were being transported to a bioweapon laboratory in Virginia, where they were set to be destroyed when the aircraft exploded mid-flight. The titanium-lined canister has a transponder of its own. The bacteria is thought to be secure and to have fallen from the wreckage, landing exactly one and a half miles east of a town called Helm's Hamlet, Iowa."

"Are we thinking this is a possible terrorist plot? How did the plane go down?"

"No, Ike. We do not believe it was a terrorist attack, but we have yet to recover the black box from the crash site."

"Why is that?"

Smith looked at Andrews and then back at Craig.

"Because you haven't recovered it yet."

## FIVE

**THE NEXT SLIDE CAME INTO** view showing a population chart for Helm's Hamlet. The population was just over six hundred people. It was a blue-collar town, rural and overrun with wheat and corn farms. There were three men for every one woman, and the average annual income was well below the national average. The next slide showed a thermal image map of the town. The entire town was void of any souls, as indicated by the light blue color illuminating the map. Everywhere except one building, the church in the town square.

Once the team had a moment to grasp the gravity of the situation, General Andrews cleared his throat, breaking the palpable silence in the room.

With a clear voice, he began to introduce the men sitting around the table. Craig knew he would be last. The team leader is always introduced last, so he sat back and studied each man as their name was called.

The first team member was introduced with the callsign Indigo. He was the short, Latino man who had asked a question during the briefing. Craig noted this and nodded at the man as their eyes met. Indigo returned the gesture as Andrews told everyone that he was on loan from Dark River. He was not the only member of the crew to be introduced in that manner. There was a black man with a thick beard, who answered to Grim, and two other guys, both white with short military haircuts and clean-shaven faces, named Salt and Tripod.

The small amount of intel thus far had him worried. Every joint CIA/military operation had an added air of danger. The intelligence was not always fully divulged and typically led to a lot of dead men and women in uniform. If all of that was normal in his line of work, the addition of a team largely composed of Dark River operatives meant this mission was completely off the books. Which meant once they were in the shit, they were on their own. When Dark River guys, based on Craig's experience, are put into a corner, everyone is considered to be hostile, everyone.

Dark River was officially listed as a "consulting" firm specializing in military-style operations, personal protection, and security for multi-billion-dollar corporations. This was all a fancy way of saying they were mercenaries. Most of their work was done overseas, largely in war-torn countries, where some of the dirtier work they did was lost in the chaos. It was rare they adhered to any kind of justice system, whether a military tribunal or a civilian court, which made them incredibly scary. Their goal was the mission. Everything and everyone else was moot. The more he ran through the history of Dark River missions that he knew of, the more concerned he became with allowing these guys to operate on United States soil.

Craig was so deep in thought about all of the ways this mission could go "tits up" in a hurry that he almost missed the final member of the team he was responsible for. A CIA field operative who introduced himself as Hawk. The young man with a nice, polite part in his hair, perfectly combed and held together with a healthy amount of hair gel, smiled and nodded to everyone around the table while playing with the knot in his tie. Craig wondered if this moron was for real. Agents never used their real names in the field, this was known and expected. This is why every agent was typically named Smith. Craig wondered if this guy chose a tough guy name because he was anything but a tough guy. Were they sneaking someone who didn't belong on the team? Having this joker on the team made a promisingly bad situation even worse. Craig was given no time to dwell on his immediate hatred for the young Hawk as he heard his own callsign being announced by the general.

"Ike, do you want to add anything?" Andrews asked.

Craig rose slowly, careful to look deep in thought as opposed to showing the pain shooting up his back and down his leg like a busy interstate. His bad hip was doing him no favors in setting the tone, but Craig thought he covered it well enough that nobody noticed. He looked around the table, solemnly studying each man before he spoke.

"I'm assuming you fellas have all worked together before," he said, pointing his fingers at each of the Dark River guys. After a quick nod, in unison just to put an exclamation point to their answer, Craig continued.

"We stay frosty out there. This should be standard. We extract the canister and get the fuck out of Dodge. If we find our initial objective is compromised, meaning the fungus has been released, our secondary objective will become the people of Helm's Hamlet."

Turning his attention back to the general, Craig asked, "I am assuming little to no resistance from the civilians?"

Before the general could speak, Grim said, "Assuming they aren't already fucking dead."

Andrews confirmed both Craig and Grim's concerns, "Yes, Ike. We expect little to no resistance. That said, this is rural Iowa. I would assume everyone is armed. Grim, yes, assuming they are not dead, we retrieve and extract the citizens of Helm's Hamlet."

Salt chimed in and said, "Well, I guess you can all see why we call him Grim..."

Craig broke up the light laughter around the table by saying, "Even with no resistance expected, should you come across anyone looking to get in our way, you will fuck them up. We got a job to do that doesn't need interruptions."

A steady chorus of testosterone-filled responses began to fill the room as Craig held up his hand to silence the jubilation. To his surprise, it had worked. Pleased that they fell in line so quickly, Craig continued.

"Fuck them up does not mean terminate them. It means hand to hand. It means to get them on the ground and out of our way. Regardless of what we're rolling into, we will not squeeze a trigger unless I give the go-ahead. Clear?"

"Yes, sir," Dark River responded in unison.

Hawk said nothing, which did not go unnoticed by Craig. The general started to speak again, the silent sign that it was time for Craig to sit back down.

"The transponder shows the target has not moved since the crash. We are going to insert you here, half a klick from the target," General Andrews said, pointing to a new satellite image of a cornfield.

"You'll drive in, escorted by a small support team in LATVs—Light Armor Tactical Vehicles. Once in place, you will retrieve the canister, and we extract you the same route with a heavy escort and helicopter overwatch."

"Sounds like a piece of cake," Hawk said with a cocky smirk on his face.

The table collectively groaned, the Dark River soldiers throwing wadded-up pieces of paper in Hawk's direction.

"If you just fucked us, I swear, boy, I will put you down like a sick dog," Salt said, all of the humor wiped from his face.

Craig chimed in, "Nobody is doing anything in the briefing room. Hawk, unless you have a question or relative intel, do us all a favor and shut the fuck up."

Hawk looked astounded, "You can't talk to me like that. I am running this operation side by side with you."

Smith rolled his eyes and exasperatedly echoed Craig's suggestion, "Hawk, shut the fuck up."

Hawk heeded the order from his superior and sank into his chair like a spoiled brat.

The general spoke up again, "If you gentlemen will follow me, we would like to show you what you'll be working with today."

The team rose and followed General Andrews as he led them through the control center. Every person in their way stopped and made a path as they walked past. Craig understood the importance of containing a biological weapon and any threat it may present, but if the canister was sealed and in a field with no issue, why was he here? Why were any of them here? This is a simple extraction. The need for secrecy is one thing, but to have some heavy hitters on a simple extraction was another. Hawk could have handled this with a couple of other senior agents. This was a lot of production for a "piece of cake." Craig knew better than to voice his concerns, though. He was already here. They all were. No use in crying about it now.

After exiting the main building, the group took a hard right and was standing in front of a heavily armored truck. The standard army green painted monster and six wheels on each side, with one large hatch at the rear of the vehicle. The hatch began to rise slowly, revealing the contents of the truck. The smells of fresh gun grease released into the open air was enough to tell Craig where they were. The armory was Craig's happy place. The unbelievable respect owed to each one of these weapons was unattainable as far as he was concerned. Not only for their ability to take a life but the complicated and efficient way they did their job was beyond reproach. To Craig, a firearm was more honest and more trustworthy than a person. All he had to do was take care of it and this beautifully deadly machine would always take care of him. Craig was unsure of how many people he could truthfully say that about.

The Dark River men looked like kids on Christmas. The weapons on display were as varied as they were glorious. The armorer saluted the general and then smiled as he turned his attention to the team.

"Gentlemen, we have some wonderful toys for you this evening. For your sidearm, we have some new standard issue eight-round .45 caliber pistols. Your primary weapon will either be a modular submachine gun or the always reliable M4. I assume this will be acceptable to everyone."

Craig was looking at paradise of firearms, the old feelings coming back to him. A smile began to form just before that sinking feeling hit him again. *Why do we need this to retrieve in a canister from a cornfield in Bum Fuck, Iowa?* The further along this operation went, the less sense it made to Craig.

Each member of the team chose the handgun to their liking, selecting their sidearm, followed by the submachine gun as their primary weapon. Hawk, unsurprisingly, decided to go with the weapons that were the biggest, choosing his sidearm and the M4 rifle. Craig was certain that this wannabe cowboy was going to get someone killed—probably himself.

The submachine gun was designed for close-quarters combat and was perfect for urban areas. This choice as your primary weapon for this operation made all the sense in the world. They expected little to no resistance so the magazine capacity could be on the shorter side. Anyone they did have to put down was likely an American citizen. It was imperative they only wounded someone at best. The submachine gun had a small caliber round which would ensure less damage to the target. Not to mention this mission was technically a military operation on American soil, overseen by the CIA. This was not legal. Finally, should the bacteria be exposed, the team would have to go into town. This meant potential urban combat against an unknown number of hostile and infected people. Again, the submachine gun was the weapon of choice.

The M4 rifle that Hawk had chosen was unnecessary. It had a larger magazine capacity, a large-caliber round, and the longer barrel made it more difficult to effectively clear a room. If you had to move around a corner, a hostile would be able to see the barrel, grab it, pull slightly, and you are off balance and exposed to multiple kill wounds from a knife. This one choice made Hawk largely unusable if they had a worst-case scenario. If he was unusable, he may as well just stay at the base. *Maybe*, Craig thought, *the kid was smarter than he gave him credit for.*

Happy to have their weapons chosen, the men working inside the armory got busy pulling, preparing, loading, and assuring the team the weapons would be waiting for them in the LATV. General Andrews escorted the team away from the armory and back into the main camp. He walked them through the various people working hard and took them into a large tent.

Once each member of the team had walked through the flaps, the general began the last portion of his briefing.

"I saved the worst for last, boys. Should the canister be compromised, we have mop suits you'll have to wear."

A collective groan was the response from everyone but Craig. Most of the team had served in Iraq at some time, and the need to wear chemical suits turned out to be an unnecessary evil, as they later found out. Should an actual firefight be necessary, their vision would be cut off by about forty percent. The breathing was difficult inside a mop suite helmet and was damn near impossible once the bullets started flying. The natural adrenaline spike and increased heart rate forced you to breathe heavier, needing more oxygen to regulate your pounding heart. Oxygen inside those fucking helmets was sparse, to say the least. It was less than optimal, but the use of the protective gear was the first piece of news Craig had heard since arriving that didn't have him worried.

As bored as he was with retirement, he had gotten used to the fact that he was going to survive. When he had first enlisted at the age of seventeen, lying about his age on the paperwork, he had made peace with the fact that he was already dead. A mindset he was convinced had not only made him an effective soldier but ended up actually saving his life. Most of the guys who carried a fear of death into battle ended up having their worst fear met. In the short time since he had been out, he had let that hard shell soften a bit. He wanted to live, which, he supposed, made him less of a soldier than he once was. Dying old sounded a lot better than dying in the mud and shit in some country nobody cared about... or in a cornfield in Helm's Hamlet, Iowa.

"You don't have to wear them until you exit the vehicles, but rest assured, gentlemen, you will wear them. We need all of you healthy and happy upon your return. Roger that?"

"Yes, General," the group, Craig included, responded immediately.

"Good. Let's get you on the road."

Once the men were at the LATVs, they each inspected their various weapons. Although the weapons were prepared by the best the US military had to offer, no true warrior let his weapon go uninspected, whether you were a Roman gladiator or the best sniper in the world.

Almost in unison, each man pulled the slide of their submachine gun back to confirm that a round was chambered. Once satisfied, they ejected the magazine and gave it a quick tap against their hips to ensure the rounds were packed tightly. With the magazine reinserted, it was the submachine gun's sights that required attention. The guns were raised, with the butt of the automatic weapons placed firmly into the crook of their shoulder. As they looked down the sights to ensure a true aim, they moved their upper bodies from left to right, locating dummy targets in the immediate area. Once satisfied with the weapon, they repeated each step for their handguns. Satisfied with their secondary weapons, each man checked their hand to hand or "dirty fighting" tools. Most of the men carried standard-issue knives with a seven-inch blade, save for Indigo and Hawk. Indigo had a spring baton he snapped to life, retracting and extending the black metal bar with a flip of his wrist. Hawk carried brass knuckles—nobody was surprised.

The final weapons check was completed within five minutes. An exercise in futility since no flaw had been found. The men loaded themselves into their light armored vehicles with Craig, Hawk, and Tripod in LATV One. Indigo, Grim, and Salt rode in LATV Two. Craig sat in the front passenger seat next to the driver the army had provided. Hawk sat behind the driver, which made Craig feel comfortable. The thought of an agency man sitting behind him gave him thoughts of every single gangster movie ever.

Indigo had taken the front passenger seat in his LATV, which gave Craig a sense of relief. Indigo seemed like the only non-cowboy in the group. That immediately elevated him to the number two on this team. Every strong team lead needed a second-in-command. With a ragtag team such as this, it was even more important to have one that has some familiarity with at least a couple team members. As long as Indigo backed Craig's call, Craig knew everyone else would back Indigo.

General Andrews's voice came through the earpieces the men had slipped into their ears the minute they had sat and situated themselves into their vehicles. As clear as the thoughts in their own heads, they heard, "Mission is a go. Good luck, gentlemen."

# SIX

**THE LATVS BEGAN TO ROLL** out of the base. The first twenty minutes of the mission went exactly to plan. The men drove down the road, quietly listening to the chatter in their ears. It was all communication between the men and women on watch duty just outside of the team's entry point. After a few moments, the vehicles made an abrupt left turn and picked up speed as they began to drive through a cornfield. The thwacking sound of the corn against the side of the vehicle started to become hypnotic, trying to disrupt Craig's focus. Once the heavy-duty tires found the proper traction and the vehicle's momentum was just right, they began to slow their pace. Military vehicles were not equipped with headlights. While it may seem counterproductive to a civilian, it was vital to maintain mission security so that you did not alert your enemy prematurely. For night driving, their appointed transportation officer was using night vision goggles. Even with the best version, which these certainly were not, they were not recommended to use at high speeds, especially in a civilian area where streetlights and other cars could literally blind you in a flash.

A satellite feed with a five-second delay was keeping General Andrews and Agent Smith apprised of the situation. They continued to monitor and give updates as to how far out the team was, whether there was movement around the canister or any potential containment breaches. Just as planned, the LATVs came to a halt exactly half a mile away from the target. The men exited the vehicles and turned on the flashlights under their primary weapons. The illumination gave the team an idea of their surroundings. It was just a shit load of corn.

The general advised the team to begin walking north-northwest before Craig called the team around for one final brief. Craig thought it was always best to keep focus on the mission. Too many times a dull mission would fail because a fight was not expected. The men would get bored quickly. Whether or not a fight was expected tonight was irrelevant. Craig was not taking the risk.

"Alright, let's listen up. Whether this is reservist work or not, it doesn't matter. We *will* go into this as professionals. We *will* get the job done. Should anything go wrong, listen for my calls. You follow my lead then drinks are on me. Heard?"

A couple "ooh rahs" shouted out in response, indicating to Craig an affirmative response that the team was already in work mode. It also told him that these boys were the cowboys he had feared. A regular soldier would be reserved at this moment, focused on their jobs, but these guys were shouting like they were attending a college football game.

Craig nodded and turned, "Let's go get this stupid fucking canister."

Andrews chimed in quickly, "Ike, I believe you're forgetting one key detail."

Craig paused and hung his head.

"Affirmative," he responded, disappointed in himself.

Without saying a word, the team turned back around, got into the rear of the vehicle, and pulled out the trunks containing their chemical suits. Once suited up, the men began their mission... again.

Exactly two minutes and twelve seconds later, the team was standing over top of their prize. Craig bent down with Hawk, both inspecting the canister. The rest of the team created a secure perimeter around Ike and Hawk by encircling them, facing away with their weapons raised at the ready. The men scanned the dark and empty cornfield for any sign of movement. Their job was to protect the men who had to lower their defenses to inspect the package. Hawk exhaled very loudly into his communicator. After a long silence, Smith nervously spoke up and asked for confirmation on the last transmission.

"All clear," Hawk excitedly responded.

"Excellent work, gentlemen. Really top-notch job," Andrews said with an evident smile on his face.

Indigo broke into the celebration solemnly, "Ike, can you take a look at this?"

Craig stood up hesitantly, having immediately registered the tone in Indigo's voice. Outside of the fact that this was the first time Craig had heard him speak a full sentence, the tone in his voice was enough to tell Craig that something was wrong. He focused his eyes on Indigo's flashlight and followed it to the illuminated target. A large, metallic object was lying on its side.

"What have you got, Ike?" Andrews asked hesitantly.

"Stand by, Oz," Craig said, using the base's callsign.

Indigo and Ike looked over the object as confused as they were afraid, not that either man was the type to admit to such a thing. They exchanged a few glances, unsure exactly how to relay this information.

"Ike, what are you looking at?" Smith asked this time.

"Unknown, stand by..." Craig responded, annoyed.

Command was always annoying when the unexpected came into a mission. It was understandable that those in charge wanted constant information since they didn't have eyes on the target. That being said, the constant chatter was a distraction for those with the actual mission. Of course, telling command to shut the fuck up for a minute was never advised.

He approached the mysterious metallic object slowly. Craig was certainly no farmer, but he could tell this thing did not belong in a field. At first glance, he thought it was a part of the aircraft that had been ripped apart. Upon closer inspection, Craig was able to tell it was definitely not part of a plane. He called the rest of the team over with Hawk holding the canister in a secured metal box by the handles on both sides. The men all shrugged their shoulders and further demonstrated their confusion by muttering a few dozen curse words. Unsure how else to explain it, he radioed back to Oz.

"Come in, Oz. This is Ike. We seem to have a sarcophagus flipped on its side," he said, equal parts confused and humored by the strange finding.

"Say again, Ike."

"We have found a coffin. Repeat, a coffin."

Smith, sounding like he just saw a ghost, asked, "Ike, this is very important. Is the package open?"

Craig's face crinkled up in a confused state before fully registering the question. *What the hell kind of question was that? Was it open? What the hell was going on?*

Indigo, standing across from Craig and at the front of the coffin, nodded his head up and down to confirm.

"Affirmative," Craig replied, "What the hell is going on?"

"Say again, Ike," Smith replied.

"Affirmative," Craig said, "The casket is open."

The silence started to become palpable before Smith finally replied, "Hawk, get the package back home. Your mission is complete. The rest of you, standby."

With a shrug of his shoulders, Hawk turned his back on the team and hurriedly made his way back the way they had come. At that moment, Craig's worst fears had been met. They were in the unforeseen. He was on an off-books mission with a team he didn't know. Now the only leverage they had just hitched a ride back to safety. As Craig hung his head, being able to see his entire short and bleak future playing out in his mind, he noticed something in the dirt. He tilted his head and brought his flashlight over the marks in the dirt. *It can't be. There has to be an explanation.*

"Oz, come in."

"We said to hold tight, Ike," Smith said angrily.

"Oz, we have footprints in the dirt."

If you could hear someone turn completely pale, Craig imagined it would sound something like Vernon Smith's voice when he replied.

"Repeat that last transmission, Ike."

Craig responded as ordered, "We have a pair of footprints. Barefoot. Leading away from the coffin."

# SEVEN
## CONFIDENTIAL

**CRAIG IMAGINED THE NEXT FEW** minutes at Oz were relatively hectic. *If they knew this coffin was supposed to be here, they did a brilliant job of hiding it,* Craig thought.

Grim had been voicing his conspiracy theories about mummies, zombies, and vampires in the downtime while Salt tried to add fuel to the fire at every chance he got. Right as Grim was about to be worked into a completely unhinged meltdown, Smith's voice broke up the drama.

"Ike, this is Oz. We've updated your mission objectives. Follow the footprints. Our guess is somebody in the area saw the crash and decided to try to make some money, or something like that."

"Oz, that's a fantastic theory that you boys have come up with. Make money off what?" Craig responded.

"I am not at liberty to divulge that information. The good news is you no longer have to wear your mop suits."

Craig wanted to respond with, "Don't bright side me, mother fucker."

Instead, he went with a monotone, "Good news. Roger that."

*Such a good little soldier,* he thought to himself sarcastically.

Andrews had the decency to wait a few seconds so the team could shed the biohazard suits and regroup before he briefed them on the details of their newest mission.

"Ike, we would like you to follow the footprints, recon the situation, and then report back to us. We'll go from there."

Craig was less than pleased by the lack of a plan, but for him, there was something exciting about the unknown. There was something exciting about how scared Agent Smith sounded. Most people would think the risk was not worth the reward here, but not Craig. To Craig, this was starting to smell like a good hunt.

The boys gathered up, and before they set off, Craig formally named Indigo his second. Given the situation they were walking into, it seemed more than appropriate to set a clear chain of command. Nobody had any objections, telling Craig he had chosen the right man, and they set off to track their prey.

The footprints led the team through the field and across the street; the muddy footprints on the asphalt allowed them to track the target into another field of tall wheat stalks. The first and most obvious thing the team noticed was the massive fire raging. It did not seem to be spreading like the wildfires raging in out west, but there was no indication the fire would be dying down anytime soon. Craig wondered, to himself, why there were no emergency services at the scene. As a matter of fact, Craig noticed for the first time that there was no sound at all save for the burning heap of metal in front of them. He knew Helm's Hamlet was a small town but was positive they had a fire department of some sort. Even his small town in Ohio had a volunteer squad. *This is all wrong*, he thought. If the rest of the team had noticed this, they had the good sense to keep it to themselves.

The team lined up single file, following the tracks around the fire. The heat coming off the burning jet was intense as they got closer to the blaze. Salt whined the most about the heat. Grim continued to bitch and moan about the lack of details provided to the unit and the secrets this proved the government had been keeping. Craig wanted them to stay focused but thought better of saying anything right now. The guys were nervous, and the bitching was a far better use of their energy than silently stewing over the cluster fuck they were walking into. There would be a time he would need to remind them to tighten up but not yet.

"Oz, we are at the crash site. Should we still recover the black box?" Craig asked.

"Negative. Follow the footprints," Smith replied.

As the tracks wound around the crash site, seemingly more than once, they straightened out and began to head toward Helm's

Hamlet's town center. A fire truck was parked with its lights flashing, but no noise other than the running engine and the faint sounds of the fire behind them was present. This was the first sign of life the team had seen since they had arrived. A collective sigh of relief quickly turned into a cold chill down the spine of each man as they got closer to the vehicles.

A massive smear of blood ran down the center of the door, covering most of the "Truck 1 Helm's Hamlet FPD" decal that took up the entire door panel. Tripod crossed himself and was the first to look away. He began searching the faces of his teammates, hoping that one of the men had an answer to the most obvious question: What the hell was going on? Unfortunately, for Tripod, nobody was saying a word.

"Oz, this is Ike. We've tracked the target to—" Craig started before he was interrupted by Indigo.

"Ike, I got military vehicles and weapons over here. I'm looking at more blood and indications of a firefight."

Craig had been so entranced by the bloodstains that he didn't realize most of the team had peeled off to start scouting the immediate area. He was slightly embarrassed, and for the first time today, he felt he was out of practice and ill-prepared for a mission, yet here he was.

"Did anyone return fire?" Craig asked.

Indigo looked behind him to the LATV, then the driver's side of the firetruck, and back to the ground. He found plenty of spent bullet casings on the ground in front of the passenger side door of the tactical vehicle. What he did not find were any bullet holes in the vehicles. This indicated one of three scenarios could have happened.

One, the soldier fighting next to the vehicle took out his target before they were able to get a shot off. If that were the case, where was the soldier?

Two, the soldier fighting was taken out by a sniper. One shot, one kill. If that were the case, why would the sniper come in to claim the body? That is not how a sniper behaves.

Three, the most terrifying option, there was nobody returning fire, and the soldier died fighting.

"Negative, sir. It looks like it was either a one-sided fight or a very accurate shooter," Indigo replied.

"Anyone got a body? Anything to indicate people were here?" Craig asked

"You mean other than the blood?" Grim shot back.

"Yes, Grim, other than the blood. Find me a body. They couldn't have gotten far."

"Maybe someone took the bodies?" Salt hypothesized.

"This isn't some eighties sci-fi action movie, you moron," Tripod responded, attempting some levity.

Grim retorted quickly, "As far as *you* know, this isn't an eighties sci-fi movie..."

"Alright God damn it. We need to tighten up," Indigo said, his voice cool and calm.

The other men quickly shut up and looked to Craig for an answer. He had no idea what to make of the situation other than to radio back to the base.

"Oz, this is Ike. Come in."

Andrews came online and asked, "Ike, what are we looking at?"

"I'll be honest, Oz. I was about to ask you the same thing. We tracked the footprints to the crash site. It appears your 'thief' looked around for something to salvage and then made their way to the main road leading into/out of town. We are looking at a local fire department truck with blood smears all over the doors and the cabin, no bodies. We have also located a military vehicle. It appears its occupants were in the process of setting up a checkpoint. There is a large amount of blood on the LATV as well a significant amount of spent 5.56mm cartridges on the ground. Again, there are no bodies. Over."

Every update Craig gave seemed to make the response time from Oz take longer and longer. He was not the only person to notice as Tripod started to complain about having his "dick out in the open" while they waited on responses. The lack of a reasonable and cohesive mission objective seemed to also be upsetting Indigo, showing frustration for the first time. Craig was about to demand some sort of answer when General Andrews finally answered back.

"We believe you've got an unknown number of hostiles pilfering the wreckage. Our concern now is for the civilians in Helm's Hamlet. Take the road into town and proceed directly to the First Presbyterian Church on 10th and Main. The latest thermal images show us no changes in the situation. Once you are at the church, radio back with details, and we'll proceed from there. Watch for hostiles."

"Roger that," Craig replied.

He knew their assessment of the situation was a joke. There was no firefight here. How would a group of hostiles be able to organize so quickly after the crash? We barely got our shit together inside of a day, and we knew the flight existed, the sensitivity of the cargo, and exactly where the crash happened. No, they were being sent on a bull shit mission with bull shit intelligence and a bull shit team. Everything about this mission was wrong.

The team was preparing to start walking when Craig called for the team to stop. He walked over to the abandoned, blood-stained LATV and looked inside the driver's side. Seeing that the interior was largely free of blood and other internal body gunk, he jumped inside. The way Craig saw it, the faster they got to town and figured this out, the sooner everyone would be home.

With all passengers secure, Craig started the engine with the push of a button, bringing the large diesel engine to life. With a roar of the engine, the team headed for the church.

# EIGHT

**THE IDEA HAD ALREADY CROSSED** his mind that the majority of this mission was being withheld from him, but the now festering thought was that his team was very quickly becoming more expendable by the second. From here on out, the team would need to proceed with extreme caution. The only thing worse than being dead was being dead because you didn't trust your instincts. Craig's instincts told him they were driving straight to their doom.

Driving a steady fifteen miles an hour, the team scanned out their windows for any potential threats. With guns raised, each passenger was looking for a target. Of course, none were found. No targets. No civilians. Not even a whisper of wind was blowing.

*If a zombie-creating bioweapon, a mysterious eight-foot coffin, and mummy-esque footprints were not enough to freak you out, the eerie silence of an entire town was certain to do the trick*, Craig thought.

Undeterred by the collective fear building up in them, the team continued to progress down Main Street with no signs of life. At this point, Craig was certain everyone was just hoping to see one survivor. Normally these guys would be looking for an enemy to eliminate. Survivors that required rescuing often got military men killed. It was not intentional, of course. It was something that occurred because civilians were not trained to store that fear. Instead, they allow it to rule them. In an emergency situation, the vast majority of people will start to run with no reason or destination in mind. They just bail. Fight or flight is usually flight.

After the complete silence of the first eight blocks, 9th Avenue started to look a little more hopeful, in that a single light was on in the upper right window of an old brick building. Craig thought about stopping, but one light was just not enough to peel off of the mission. The objective was the church, not to clear out some random room in the upstairs of Nate's Ye Olde Hardware Store, as the sign read.

Craig stayed focused but was still very unsure of how they would proceed. For obvious reasons, churches are very sacred to a majority of people. It is thought to be far worse to commit a crime in a church than anywhere else, except maybe a hospital. That being the case, five guys armed to the hilt in all black storming into a church was a very bad look. Beyond that, it also made no tactical sense. If the intel was correct, there could be an unknown number of targets holding a large portion of the town hostage in a contained small space they didn't know the layout of. Looking at the church now, Craig thought to himself, *this was a recipe for a cluster fuck if ever there were one.*

Ready or not, it's go time. Like it or not, he was the quarterback. The entire point of Craig's existence on this mission started right now. He took a deep breath while looking at the church. This seasoned military veteran studied the brick-and-mortar structure up and down and from side to side, like a drunk checking out a girl in a bar. Following a deep inhale through the mouth and a steady exhale through the nostrils, his standard mind-clearing exercise, Craig was ready to call the play.

"Okay, listen up. Indigo and Grim, flank left. Check the side windows first. If they are too tall, someone is giving somebody a boost up. Figure it out. I want eyes on the inside. We're looking for signs of life. Any movement is a green light to enter. If we can't confirm, continue to work your way around back. Look for entry points and possible traps. Make your way back around to me. Salt and Tripod, you're covering their six. If you see something, don't just open fire. Rules of engagement are sticky at best right now. Do not fire unless fired upon. I'll stay here covering the main entrance. Under no circumstances do we proceed inside right now. I want to get in there, but I also want a hell of a lot more information before we storm the church. Heard?"

"Roger that, boss," Indigo said, slapping Grim's shoulder.

Indigo gave a tilt of his hand, telling Grim to follow. Grim looked like he was about to say something, but he decided a deep sigh was better and turned to follow Indigo.

The four made their way around the building and out of Craig's sight. He adjusted his earpiece appropriately to ensure he wouldn't miss even the faintest of whispers. Confident he had the optimal listening experience, he proceeded cautiously toward the massive wooden front doors of the church. Craig studied the door frame at length as if he was a carpenter. Craig, however, was not admiring the craftsmanship of the old oak doors but was looking for wires, a camera, or even the ominous blinking red light. There was nothing. For all intents and purposes, the church doors were safe for people to come and go as they pleased.

Craig pressed on the wrought-iron door handle with the slightest of ease. As the door gave, he heard no alarms, clicks, or any sounds that may indicate his impending death. The door gave a bit more and creaked loudly. Craig jumped back, almost falling off the front steps. Regaining his balance, he raised his weapon and waited. Nothing. It was the same creepy silence that had been following them since the fires in the wheat field. Once the adrenaline began to leave his body, he could feel the pain in his hip sending shockwaves through his body. He felt a hand grasp his shoulder from behind and spun, about to depress the trigger, when he saw a pencil-thin mustache on his would-be assailant's upper lip.

"God damn it, Indigo. You scared the shit out of me!"

"My bad, Ike. We heard the door open and came running. You were frozen like you saw something, so we lined up to cover you. It was only after a minute of you just standing there like a fucking statute that I decided to approach."

Composing himself, Craig placed a hand on Indigo's shoulder and said, "Damn it, Indigo. Uncle Ike could never be mad at you."

The team chuckled, and Craig considered his deflection to have been a success. The last thing he wanted to show was his age, ailments, or alarm to this group. The more of a blank canvas he was, the better. He'd had friends in this business before and didn't need to disappoint anyone else.

"What do you got for me?" Craig asked.

"Nada," Indigo replied.

"Nothing?"

"Ike, we didn't see shit. We both took turns trying to look inside. That stained glass is some blurry shit," Grim said.

"Okay... well, the front door is open. I don't like it, but we didn't come all this way to just window shop, did we? Let's see who is home," Craig said.

Looking back at the small crack in the door frame, the light from inside the holy site shining out into an otherwise dark night, Craig thought he'd like to ponder on the metaphor. Unfortunately, along with not being here to stand around, he also wasn't here to find God. It was time to go to work.

"I'll be primary. Grim, you follow me and clear left."

"Fuck yeah," Grim replied, nodding at Craig and checking the slide of his submachine gun one last time to ensure that a round was still chambered.

Craig turned his attention to Salt. "You'll be third and will clear the right."

"Yes, sir," Salt replied with the same cocky smirk he wore during most of the briefing back at Oz.

"Indigo..."

Indigo knew what his job was and made sure everyone else did too.

"I'm covering the rear. Roger that, boss."

"Good," Craig said as he nodded in approval.

"Looks like it's time to confess our sins," Tripod said.

"That's Catholics, dipshit," Indigo quickly shot back

"Well, what is this?"

"It's Presbyterian," Grim said.

"What's Presbyterian then?"

A brief silence lay over the five men, with nobody being able to answer that question with anything other than a shoulder shrug. Clear that this would not be solved tonight, the team lined up behind Craig, ready to go to work. Indigo was the first to signal he was ready by placing his left hand on Tripod's left shoulder. Tripod followed by placing his hand on Salt, Salt to Grim, and

Grim touching Craig's shoulder. With a squeeze of Grim's left hand, Craig began to move steadily toward the church with his gun raised.

# NINE

**THE DOOR CREAKED OPEN WITH** a bit of pressure applied by Craig's large left hand. The horror movie-like creak of the door opening would have been scary as hell on a normal day but was of no relevance right now. Fear was no longer a factor. Within the blink of an eye, they were all prepared. Craig moved in with steady purpose, left foot first with his right firmly planted behind, the ball of his foot never touching the ground, each step following suit in a smooth continuous motion. This was no different from a well-choreographed ballet.

The first thing he noticed was the intense heat and smell. It didn't smell or feel like a fire. This was like someone kept the heater running all day at eighty degrees and left raw chicken out on the counter. Each step they took allowed the rancid smell of a meat processing plant to overcome most of their senses. Eyes watering, mouth salivating as nausea swept over them, they continued to move through the atrium.

Each member of the team would tell Craig an area or corner was cleared and then continue to move forward, realigning to enter the main chamber. Salt and Indigo broke off to the left and the right and positioned themselves to throw back a large red theater curtain, by the split in the middle, that separated the church's atrium from the chapel. Both men looked at Craig for permission. He nodded his head in approval then the curtain was thrown back.

Craig took two steps forward but paused. Grim and Tripod broke off to the right and left, respectively, but stopped midway through their first step. It suddenly became clear to Craig what that rancid smell was. The air in this sanctuary was rife with the scent of piss, shit, vomit, and the hot, rotting corpses that used to be the people of Helm's Hamlet, Iowa. Every seat in every pew was filled with a different citizen. Although, to be fair, some citizens had body parts in multiple seats. The walls of the church were splattered in dark-red, dried blood. The corpses that sat in pews, most of them appearing to be looking up to the heavens. While it was a nice thought, they did not appear to be doing so to get closer to God. It was more likely due to the fact that their heads had been almost detached at the throat.

"Holy shit," Grim muttered.

Craig was momentarily shocked by the carnage in front of him. He'd seen villages in Africa ravaged by rival religious groups. He'd seen Muslims commit genocide against other Muslims because of the differences in how they worshiped Allah. He had never seen anything like this. This scene seemed to be staged like someone wanted them found in this way.

This thought snapped Craig back to reality, and he started to put some of the pieces together. The thermal reading showed warm bodies. Dead bodies do not give off heat. The temperature in the church had been raised. This felt like an ambush. On full alert, Craig raised his gun back up to level with his eye line.

"Snap to damn it. This is all wrong. We don't have the time to be appalled right now. This was done to fuck with us. Move forward, look for survivors or anything that can tell us what happened here," he told his team.

As ordered, the crew gathered their composure, reminded themselves that they were professionals, and raised their guns to proceed with the mission.

Each member broke off in their own direction and started working each pew from the back of the church to the front, winding through each row in a serpentine fashion. The number of bodily fluids contaminating the floor made it difficult for anyone to move with any kind of speed or balance. The soft and tactical movement they had earlier was now sacrificed for flat-footed and unsure steps, like walking on ice. Craig hollered for the men to switch from their primary weapon to their sidearms. Once again, in unison, the guns were safetied and slung across their backs. They drew their pistols, raised them, and began to move forward a little easier. While the submachine gun they had was ideal for small spaces, this was no longer the primary concern. The team, should anything happen, would be about as close as humanly possible, making the sidearm they each held the best option.

Fifteen pews into the massacre and the continued silence from the deceased congregation was clearly enough for Tripod.

"Hello!" he shouted.

He repeated his call a second later, this time with his hands around his mouth, forming a makeshift bullhorn. Silence was all they heard in return.

Craig was annoyed at the jump scare and didn't appreciate Tripod cutting through the tedious work of examining more than two hundred corpses for any signs of life. If this were an ambush, he might have just told everyone their location. Tripod basically became the human equivalent of headlights on a LATV.

He knew he could verbally assault his subordinate for breaking silence, an egregious violation of protocol, but Craig was sick and tired of being there too. Tripod seemed to have saved them a bit of time. On board with the new plan, Craig tried one more tactic in case anyone was scared to answer back to the first voice they heard.

"We're with the United States military! This is Captain Craig Eitel. If you can hear me, please come out. We are here to help!"

Dejected, Craig turned to leave the disgusting mass murder scene when he heard a whimper.

He turned excitedly and shouted, "Make noise! We'll come to you!"

This time, a louder whimper came from underneath the minister's altar. The team sprinted toward the area to find their survivor. Their one glimmer of hope. After a little rustling around, Grim was able to move some debris callously thrown in the way and pulled back a tiny curtain. Inside, a little girl was huddled and staring back at Grim with bloodshot eyes. Her face was only clean where the tears had streamed down her cheeks and fell from her face. Everywhere the salty water hadn't touched was covered in blood, dirt, and muck. Grim, despite his hard exterior, was able to talk the girl out of her hiding space with some sweet words and the cherry-flavored hard candy in his pocket.

Fresh out of her hiding spot, Craig and Grim gave the little girl a once-over. She had dried blood that appeared to have come from her ear. She had some black substance that had covered her face, which the team originally took for her blood. She seemed dehydrated, at the least, and borderline in shock. The girl's breathing was erratic, but she appeared to be in good physical condition, aside from a scratch or two on her arms. Craig asked only once what had happened. The child recoiled halfway back into her hiding spot before Grim was able to grab her and hold her close to his chest, whispering that everything would be okay.

Craig ordered the team to escort the girl back to the Light Armor Tactical Vehicle and wait for him outside. Grim told the child to keep her eyes closed, not wanting her to see the carnage, especially if anyone in the pews had been her parents. He stood up with her in his arms and began to walk out of the church. She clung her arms tightly around his neck and closed her eyes tight, as she was told. The team instinctively flanked Grim and began to escort their cargo out of the church. Craig hung back, realizing he had yet to brief General Andrews or Smith.

"Oz, this is Ike. Over."

Andrews answered him hurriedly, "Ike, we were getting worried about you guys. You got a progress report for me, son."

"We found one survivor. A little girl, some hearing damage and light abrasions. Inside the church, we found approximately two hundred civilians. Men, women, and children. All deceased. We have seen zero hostiles. Repeat, zero hostiles. Over."

Craig heard static for a second and then his comm went dead. He was about to continue reporting when he heard Tripod shout in terror.

# BEHIND-THE-SCENES OPERATIONS

# TEN

**CRAIG LOOKED UP AND SAW** the team falling back, with Indigo firing multiple rounds at an unseen target outside of the church. The rest of the team made it back inside hurriedly and panting far too hard for the fifteen seconds they had been gone and the three yards they had to run. He heard a loud grunt, the same creaking from the front doors, and the heavy sound of them slamming shut. The look on Craig's face was enough to make Salt begin to explain.

"Sir, we stepped out of the church and were almost completely surrounded. At first, Grim thought they were other survivors until they started hissing and growling."

"They hissed and growled?" Craig asked, completely unamused.

Tripod responded hurriedly. "Fuckin' A they hissed."

I holstered my sidearm and drew my primary only to use the flashlight. I'm telling you, sir. Whatever these fuckers are, they aren't human."

"Okay—" Craig started, raising his hands up trying to calm Tripod down.

Tripod made it clear that he was not interested in calming down, however, so Craig moved on to Indigo, who had returned to the group.

"We all saw the same thing, Ike. They sure as shit looked human, but they ain't. This is the exception to the quack like a duck rule."

Indigo had to stop and collect himself with a few deep breaths. Visibly shaken, he continued.

"We all put our lights on them. At first, they recoiled a bit, like they thought it would hurt them. When they realized the light wasn't painful, they stood back up and let us get a good look at them. Most of them are torn the fuck up, like these ashy mother fuckers have chunks of skin missing, limbs missing, half the damn face looks torn off, but they were very much alive. Then they bared their teeth..."

"What?" Craig asked, on the edge of his seat. He was still confident that this was an inappropriate prank, but he was damned if Indigo couldn't spin a story.

"They had fangs. Like a wolf or a vampire."

"I fucking told y'all," Grim called back, watching the front doors of the church with his submachine gun at the ready.

"Yeah..." Indigo continued, "I know how it sounds. Except these assholes had fangs on the top and bottom of their mouths. That ain't no vamp I've ever seen on TV."

Craig was officially convinced; this was all a ruse. A poorly timed one as well, especially considering the little girl they were responsible for and the death that desecrated the church. Did these psychos from Dark River have no moral code at all? Grim had almost fooled him by showing compassion for that little girl, but this now was verging on inhumane, forget funny.

"Okay, guys, I'll bite," Craig said with a chuckle, impressed with himself over the pun.

He started to walk to the door when Indigo jumped in his way.

"Sir, I cannot allow you to open those doors."

Craig looked down at the man he dwarfed, somewhat amused by the bravado. *These guys are really going for it. Got to hand it to them,* Craig thought.

"Calm down. I'm just going to have a little look." Craig said as he moved around Indigo without incident.

He walked confidently to the front doors and saw a tiny window on both sides of the large doors. He took a look but could not see much of anything out of the poorly tinted windows. Indigo was not in a position to give him orders, Craig reminded himself, so with one big pull, the left side of the doors opened with the same creak that had become all too familiar to Craig at this point. His eyes adjusted to the darkness and saw at least twenty-four silhouettes surrounding the church, his visual confirmation aided only by the moonlight.

Craig lifted his rifle just as the team had, his flashlight washing over the group. As the creatures recoiled just as Indigo described, Craig was able to get a look at the things blocking their path to the LATV. They all looked human enough; they were even wearing clothes, some tattered and others covered in an unknown black substance, blood, dirt, or mud. As his gaze made its way from the feet up, studying everything he could about these things, he had to pause when he started seeing the difference between them and the human beings they used to be.

Their shoulders were extraordinarily broad, extending about six inches on each side. The arms attached looked more like a crab claw than they did human arms. The area above the elbow was normal enough, but the elbows seemed locked at a ninety-degree angle while the lower arm seemed to have grown almost a foot. Their large hands and long fingers paled in comparison to their long, very sharp-looking, black nails. Ike continued to move the light up reluctantly and noted their pale, flaky skin, wondering if that had something to do with why they were afraid of the light. Their heads were void of any hair, and their eyes were as black as a moonless night. Their mouths were chapped and raw.

The flashlight in their face seemed to piss them off. In unison, like a well-trained military unit, they barred their teeth, showing two small fangs where the upper incisors should have been. Craig could see something growing out of the bottom of their gums, where the bottom front four teeth would have been located. A few seconds later, a new set of fangs had fully grown. They all had their mouths open, four fangs bared, knees slightly bent, and appeared to be readying themselves in an attack position.

He could hardly believe what he was seeing. Instinctively, he depressed the trigger. His submachine gun began to ring out in the night. The muzzle flash, lighting up the otherwise black night, was also helping to keep the other creatures at bay. Within seconds, Craig noticed the team was next to him. All of them indiscriminately fired their automatic weapons into the gathered crowd of hostiles.

The creatures all screamed out in pain as they fell to the ground from the massive amount of 9mm rounds shredding their internal organs. Gaping wounds were gushing a dark, thick fluid that Craig saw was not normal human blood. The team had run through their full magazines and were in the process of reloading as they noticed movement on the ground. They had completely plowed the field, and yet every single one of the twenty-four creatures were pulling themselves to their feet. The team froze. Each man was in complete awe over what was happening. The creatures had risen, ironically, in front of a church, and in sync, all crouched low, knees bent, and arms stretched out, permanently bent at the elbows. They were in an attack position again and shrieked loudly in a horrifying falsetto.

"Fall back!" Craig shouted as they made their way back into the church, one by one.

Craig was halfway in the door, all other men having already made it safely inside, when he noticed Tripod was still firing into the oncoming crowd of beasts. Before he could make a move to grab him, Tripod's exposed left flank was being overrun. The doors closed with Craig seeing his fallen teammate being consumed by something that resembled the human equivalent of a rabid jungle cat. They had just incurred a casualty and were completely stranded. Craig was suddenly reminded why he had retired... he was the only one who didn't think he was expendable.

# ELEVEN

**CRAIG SPOKE ONCE AGAIN INTO** the microphone embedded in his earpiece.

"Oz, this is Ike. Over."

The static seemed to confirm what he already knew. They were alone. It was time for that flight or fight response, but contrary to his modus operandi, not only was he in flight mode, but he was in interstellar travel mode. He was genuinely terrified and had no plan or really any other thought than getting the hell out of there. This, however, was counterproductive to getting out of there. He could not transform into a full coward this quickly. He repeated his breathing exercises five or six times before he felt some sort of normal brain function return to him. This is what separated Craig from other people in his profession. It wasn't just blind swinging to stay in the match. Craig understood that panic was the death of success. You develop a plan that will result in the least amount of danger for you and your team. With precision, ruthlessness, and with a calmness rarely achieved outside of a day spa, dispatch any and all enemy combatants. There was no other choice.

Salt was on his own mic, attempting to reach anyone back at Oz. All he was met with was the same static Craig got. The static was the most insulting part to Craig. He'd been abandoned in the field before, and it happens more often than most people would be comfortable knowing. The particular communication system they used only created static if someone held down the microphone button at headquarters at the same time you were speaking. Someone inside Oz was making sure the team could not provide updates or obtain an extraction. Craig knew he was going to survive this... if for only long enough to figure out who decided to fuck them with no lube.

"Listen up, guys. We are in some real thick shit, and we can't expect any help from Oz. We need to work together. If we can, we will get out of here. You're good soldiers, and now that we have some sort of intelligence on these... things. I think we can at least get past them."

"Get past them? Are you fucking crazy, man? All we know is how it feels to waste time and ammunition," Salt interrupted.

Craig knew he would lose them soon if they did not start to move.

"That's a fair point, Salt. That being said, we know a couple other things. Especially about these mother fuckers. First, they are organized and attack together. The fact that they are not trying to get in here right now tells me they only attack on command. Who is controlling them... or what? I don't know. I also have no intention of finding out."

"Fuckin' A right," Salt chimed in.

"Second thing we know about them is that while they don't die when shot, they do fall down. I clocked approximately twenty seconds from the time they dropped until they stood back up. Another ten seconds and they were ready to attack. Thirty seconds is a long time in a situation like this. Finally, they are afraid of the light. We don't know if it will actually hurt them, but when I flashed my light on them, they flinched. You said they did the same thing to you, right?"

Indigo and Salt nodded. Grim was holding the little girl, who was crying once again, and whispering in her ear. Craig imagined he was telling her everything would be okay. Grim was as good of a liar as he was a man, it seemed. Craig had the plan still forming in his head, but with time being a bit of an issue, a mostly formulated plan was better than nothing.

"Timing will be the key here. First, hit them with your lights again. When they recoil, we lay down fire. Concentrate all efforts on those in our direct path to the LATV. If we do this correctly, we may be able to drive right the fuck out of here. Let Oz blow this place to hell as far as I'm concerned. Are we on board?"

A reluctant group of nodding heads answered Craig, all bravado stripped from these hardened warriors. He looked at them worried that any hesitation would cause another casualty, but he could not think of anything else that could get them out of the church and on the road back to Oz safe and sound.

"When we open the doors, the three of us will lay down suppressing fire. Grim, when the creatures fall, you take that little girl and haul ass to the vehicles. Once you have her loaded in the backseat, I expect you to begin laying down covering fire from the LATV. This may confuse them if they are receiving rounds from in front and behind them. Indigo will go next, followed by Salt, then myself. Nobody stops to wonder if a target is really down or not. You run like hell until you are at the LATV. Indigo, you're driving. I don't care if it is in reverse. Get us the fuck out of here. I'll take the front passenger seat. Salt and Grim, once you are loaded into the vehicle, don't quit firing. I don't want a single round in any of the weapons when we get back to base."

With the plan set and everyone as ready as they were going to be, Grim held the little girl tighter in his arms and started to prepare for his run. Craig, being the last man to go, advised he would open the heavy church doors. The team would flood out, blind firing until they could see a path to the vehicle. The doors flew open thanks to the adrenaline flowing through Craig's body at that moment.

Salt and Indigo poured out of the door and began firing just as instructed. They shouted for Grim to run as the first six creatures hit the ground. Grim flew out of the doors like a bird that had been trapped for days. He made it to the LATV, threw the little girl into the back seat, and began firing his submachine gun into the crowd from behind them.

Salt had to reload when Indigo made his run. The lack of covering fire caused one of the beasts to launch itself at the short Latino man. With a flip of his wrist his baton extended, and he cracked the creature's skull. A hideous cracking thud followed by a squirt of black liquid from its skull landed in Indigo's left eye. He screamed in pain but never stopped moving and made it to the vehicle. With only one eye, he struggled to reload his own weapon as quickly as necessary in order for Salt to begin his run. Craig was able to cycle his weapon quickly but had run out of rounds already for his submachine gun and had to switch to his M11. Despite the smaller weapon, Craig's accuracy did not waiver.

Salt had a considerably easier time making it back to the vehicle. Indigo advised Salt that he would need to drive because of his wounded eye. Salt confirmed the request and the two men switched positions at the LATV, with Salt moving around the vehicle and getting in front of the driver's side door. Instead of reloading when he ran dry, Salt opened the door and started the LATV.

"Get in!" Salt shouted.

Grim and Indigo complied and threw themselves into the back seat, almost knocking heads. They quickly sat up and began to fire into the crowd again, clearing a path for Craig.

Craig was at the foot of the stairs as he began to run. Suddenly he saw the LATV backing up with the thick tires squealing in a cloud of white smoke. Before he knew what had happened, he was alone. Quickly realizing the peril he found himself in, he turned to see the bodies of the recently shot starting to rise. He mumbled a curse and hoped his hip would hold up as he began to sprint down Main Street.

Craig made it less than a block before he heard the screeching coming from behind him and tried like hell to find another gear to run faster in. He assumed these creatures were fast, but he was about tapped out. He hoped they were maybe slower than he thought but was quickly disappointed when the thunderous sound of the creatures made him feel like he was running with the bulls in Pamplona. He took a chance that they were unable to turn when running at such quick speeds and cut down an alley on his right. He was granted a brief reprieve and took the opportunity to catch his breath. If his hip was sore, he could not feel it over the pounding of his heart and burning in his lungs. The sound was so loud to him that he covered his heart with his right hand as if he were saying the pledge of allegiance. He took three deep breaths and was able to steady his heart rate. He was about to check to see if the coast was clear when he heard a glass bottle being lazily kicked down the alley. Based on his luck today, Craig was not surprised that a straggler had wandered down the alley.

He froze for a moment, exposed, before he ducked behind a large dumpster. He didn't think the creature had seen him, but he heard it sniffing, as if trying to sense something, before hissing loudly. Craig drew his knife, afraid the sound of his gun would bring more of the monsters into his relatively safe alley. He sat there, eyes closed, listening for sounds to indicate how close the creature was to him. The sound of a glass bottle being kicked again broke the silence as the bottle rolled into the front right wheel of the dumpster Craig was hiding behind. He opened his eyes and saw a left foot stepping onto the freshly broken glass.

Without a sound, Craig ferociously sprang up from his crouched position, jamming the knife up the creature's mouth through the bottom of the jaw. The nine-inch blade slid into the creature's flesh like melted butter. He continued to push the blade up until the sound of the tip of the blade hit the inside of the creature's skull. The *ting* sound it made was satisfying to Craig but was not the sound of victory.

The creature, somehow still alive, tried to open its mouth with the knife still inside and Craig could smell the copper smell of blood on its breath. Although he really did not want to look, Craig opened his eyes and saw the humanoid had flesh hanging from its teeth. It was completely hairless, and the creature's pale skin seemed to be a result of incredibly dry skin, like they took a bath in an old campfire, completely covered in ash.

Craig quickly withdrew the knife and stabbed the creature again, this time in its left eye. He left the knife in as he used both of his thumbs to gouge out the creature's right eye. It popped, like a zit, without much trouble, and the creature collapsed. Craig pulled his thumbs from the oozing right eye socket and flung some of the gunk off of his hands. Knowing he had no real time to investigate this thing, Craig pulled the knife from its left eye and began to crudely cut back and forth at the monster's neck, using the jugular vein as his start and finish line.

He looked at the body of the monster and noticed it was wearing a letterman jacket from Helm's Hamlet High School. In cursive writing, on the left breast, his name was written. The black liquid pouring out of the thing made it difficult to see clearly, but this was once a person named Todd. This was once a person. Just a regular, everyday kid. Now he was sawing poor

Todd's head off with a knife. If he were a praying man, Craig would have said something for the soul of this kid. Since he wasn't, though, Craig decided that he would do the next best thing. He promised Todd that he would find everyone responsible for allowing this to happen, and he would punish them all.

After a few minutes of work and reflection, Craig bounced back up on his feet. He sat the human head, formerly known as Todd, on top of the dumpster's closed lid and waited. After a few minutes of silently watching the corpse for any kind of movement, Craig was satisfied. Decapitation seemed to be the first confirmation that these things could be killed. Happy for the first time since he had thrown Jimmy Spaski into the door of his security vehicle, Craig smiled. He had finally collected some semblance of reliable intelligence on what they were dealing with. Now, he needed some proper shelter to wash the thick black blood of the creature off and catch his breath. Shortly later, he began to run out of the alley toward the only place he could think of.

# TOP SECRET
# TWELVE

**CRAIG ARRIVED AT HIS DESTINATION** a few seconds after sneaking out of the alley, the blackout in town playing a significant role in concealing him. He was back on 9th Avenue looking up at the only light in town. He glanced around one last time and broke the glass front door of Nate's Ye Olde Hardware Store as quietly as possible. Reaching his hand through the freshly formed hole in the glass, careful not to cut himself, he turned the deadbolt lock over before moving his hand down to the doorknob and twisted the smaller lock as well. Craig carefully pulled his hand out of the hole and softly opened the door before slipping inside the building, locking the door behind him. It seemed stupid to Craig, but he didn't know if these creatures could figure out locks and doors. They never tried to enter the church since the doors remained closed. He knew he was grasping at straws, but Craig, forever the soldier, knew any intelligence he could gather was only going to increase the odds of him getting out of this.

He tiptoed through the hardware store, minding every step he took. He stopped to pick up a crowbar, which he tucked into his belt. He was running very low on ammo, so blunt objects were better than nothing. He had used all of the rounds in the submachine gun and discarded it for the rebar he found in aisle four. The crowbar he figured he would need to use to jimmy a door or, in the worst-case scenario, smack a creature upside the head the next time it thought about eating him. Craig figured he could use the rebar as a spear or at least something to help him keep his distance from these man-eating fuckers. If he could be honest with himself, he would find that he already knew these "weapons" were a futile attempt. Should Craig actually come across more than one of these creatures, he wouldn't stand a chance.

After rummaging through the aisles, he found the back stairs to the building, which he surmised would lead him to the mysterious illumination on the second floor. The crowbar immediately came in handy as Craig had to pry the locked door that was separating the main floor from a short staircase. Craig popped it open and listened for a minute. No noise whatsoever. No creatures stirring outside. Nobody was running around upstairs. This was either going to be a massive mistake or present a much-needed moment for him to rest and figure out what the hell his next move would be.

Craig looked at the door separating him from the light on the other side. He tried the doorknob as quietly as possible, and to his surprise, the door just opened. As he pushed the door the rest of the way open, Craig found himself staring down the wrong end of a double-barreled shotgun.

"Say something," a voice on the other end of the gun said curtly.

"Something."

"Well, at least you ain't one of them things. They can't talk, ya know," an elderly man said as he lowered his gun.

"I met a few of them. They can't talk and won't die," Craig said, too tired to care if this guy was a risk to him or not.

"Hmph, damn hippies and their drugs. I thought you was one of 'em when you broke in. Another hippy coming to rob an old man. You aren't, though. I can tell. You're here to save us."

"Who is *us*? Are there other survivors here?" Craig asked, still trying to grasp his new surroundings

"The town. You're here to save the town, right? I guessed you're military by your build. Am I the last one to be evacuated? I told them people we won't leave when the good Lord sends a tornado our way. We ain't evacuating because of some dope freaks."

"Mister, I can assure you these aren't drug-addicted teens. These things are something completely different. How many people are here with you?"

"I don't care what you call 'em, young feller. We ain't leavin'!"

"I'm sorry, sir, but there is no evacuation. We are the only people in town left. I'm truly sorry, but even I was abandoned here."

Craig thought the man was going to start crying based on the quiver in his chin, but the old man held off. He instead mumbled some nonsensical curse words as he turned, walked into the small living room, and sat down in a big leather recliner. Craig followed him into the living area but found there was no place for him to sit. He looked around and decided the floor was better than one more minute on his feet. The old man, who had yet to introduce himself, picked up a day-old newspaper and started reading the front page.

"Sir, my name is Captain Craig Eitel. Can you tell me when this started?"

He sat there for a minute, still reading his paper, before he looked up with tears in his eyes.

"My wife was on Main Street when it happened. I heard the plane crashin' from inside the store. I was convincing Ned Bowers to buy a bigger jack for that gaudy new truck he bought. He was always buying stuff. Liked to flash his money around and I didn't mind that cocky sum bitch spending his money in my store. Ned was an asshole. Now he's dead, you say? No... no, that's not possible. I saw Ned outside three hours ago. Ned, Bonnie, Larissa, and a whole mess of them boys and their guns. They walked right past my shop like it was just another day."

"Sir, the plane crash?" Craig urged him, trying desperately to mine the details from the ramblings of this elderly man.

"Oh, yes. Sorry, son, I forget where I'm at in my stories. Anyway, the plane crashed, so I runned outside to see everyone on the street all crying in pain. Half the damn town, just lying there. I found Helen, but she was unconscious. I was so scared I didn't know what to do, and nobody was helping us. Folks who weren't on the ground were running around like damned chickens with their heads cut off. I ran back to the store and got one of my large, flat carts. You know, the carts you'd use for lumber. You look like a man's man, son. You woodwork? I like to whittle, but I can't do too much these days. Damn hands."

"Sir, the plane crash?"

"Yes, I know, you impatient bastard. Anyway, I was able to scoop her up on my cart. She's in the bedroom sleeping now. She's been sleeping since we got back. I'm sure she's fine. My Helen, she's a fighter."

"I'm glad to hear that she'll be okay, sir. Can you tell me when the creatures came out?"

"Creatures?"

"Sorry, sir. The drug-addled hippies?"

"Oh, those shits came out after dark. The town was quiet because of the crash and the tornado sirens. With the number of our own people hurt, everyone not hunkered down in place was at the hospital. I heard screams when the sun had been down for about an hour. I started hearing gunfire and explosions outside, so I just locked the doors and stood guard. If any of those bastards think they're going to get Helen, they've got another thing coming. I even turned on my lamp here so they would know I am here and ain't afraid."

"You're a tough old bastard. I believe you'll protect her very well."

"Damn right. Koreans didn't kill me. No hippy can either. Say, could you give her a quick look, son? I just own a hardware store. Do you want to know what kind of socket wrench you need? I'm your guy. Well, maybe not so much anymore. I forget nowadays, but I never knew about that medical stuff."

"Of course," Craig said as he rose from his position on the ground.

He looked at his hands, realizing again they were covered in blood from the creature and desperately needed them clean— especially if he was going to be giving someone any type of medical exam.

"I need to wash my hands before I look in on anyone. Would you mind, sir?"

The old man motioned to the hallway behind him. There were two doors on either side of the small corridor. Craig opened the door on his right and saw a small bathroom with shaving cream, a razor, and a washcloth sitting on the sink. A small drip was falling from the spout every few seconds. Craig picked up the well-used, off-white bar of soap from the porcelain sink and turned on the hot water. Placing his hands under the water, he began to furiously scrub the soap between his hands. The lather was slow at first but built as more of the now steaming water combined with the soap. Soon, the drain was busy accepting the dead creature's blood and Craig's hands were as clean as could be. The same could not be said for the sliver of soap that was left, and Craig tossed it into the wastebasket nestled between the sink and toilet.

"On the left, I said!" the old man shouted from his chair.

*No, you didn't,* Craig thought, but he kept it to himself. After drying his hands on the towel hanging on the rack behind him, he closed the door, turned one hundred eighty degrees, and opened the door on the left-hand side of the hallway. Instantly confused, Craig took a step out of the bedroom to see if there were any other doors in the hallway. There were not. Craig poked his head back into the room and confirmed what he thought he had first seen. The bed was empty. There was no one in the entire room.

"Well, how is she?" the old man asked directly behind him.

He looked at Craig and then the bed and back to Craig once again. The look on the old man's face went from confusion, to fear, to anger, then finally back to confusion.

"Where is she? Where is my Helen? What did you do to her?"

Craig heard the fear in the man's voice and realized the man had to be suffering from Alzheimer's disease. Immediate regret entered Craig's mind. This mission has been nothing but a cluster fuck from the start. As cold as it seemed, Craig didn't have time to deal with this man and his disease. Before he could say anything else, the old man tore out of the bedroom and grabbed the shotgun sitting next to the front door of the tiny apartment.

"Sir, where are you going? You can't go out there."

"I don't care, damn it. They got my Helen. I'm gonna get her back."

Craig made a move to put his hand on the old man's shoulder, but with a speed that Craig didn't think was possible, the old man turned and pointed the gun in the face again. Craig was getting tired of this routine and swore, old man or not, suffering or not, the next person to point a gun at him was going to experience a uniquely unpleasant death.

"Stay back. Do not stop me," the old man said with unexpected ferocity.

Craig simply put his arms in the air as he watched the old man open the door and start running down the flight of stairs. He heard him step on the broken glass around the door frame Craig had broken open and then he was gone.

Craig locked the door behind him and took the liberty of sitting down in the old man's chair. The exhale that followed seemed to bring the day's events back to him in a flash. Trying to grasp everything he had seen was too much. He had been perfectly comfortable smoking a cigar by his pool, trying to live with his guilt before he was lured like a fish straight into an actual waking nightmare. An actual nightmare in which he was being chased by monsters. Monsters that wanted to eat him. The bodies in the church, discovering monsters exist, being abandoned by not only headquarters but his team on the ground and, of course, decapitating one of the ashy fucks.

"I'm not sure how much more of this we can take, Ike," he said aloud to himself.

Exhaustion consumed him as he rubbed his eyes. Instinctively, he reached for the lever on the reclining chair and pulled. The soft mechanical chair slammed back as Craig fell with it, laying horizontal. As he drifted off to sleep, Craig wondered if the others made it back to Oz with the little girl. Despite their betrayal, that little girl was innocent. She deserved to live, even if the rest of them didn't.

# THIRTEEN
## CONFIDENTIAL

**"GET IN!"** Salt yelled. When he heard the doors behind him close, he put the LATV in reverse and began to peel out down the road. Indigo and Grim were both yelling something about Ike, but Salt knew he had to get the fuck out of there.

As far as he was concerned, he didn't even know Ike. He was some team lead they brought in. Expendable like the rest of them. This was survival of the fittest and Ike drew the short straw, Salt rationalized to himself. When he was at least one hundred yards away from the ruckus, he slowed the vehicle down slightly and spun the wheel. An agonizing, stomach-turning second later, the vehicle was facing the same way they were traveling for the first time since they had left the church. Salt put the vehicle into drive and drove off again, making his way for anywhere but there.

Once he had calmed down, he could hear Indigo yelling in his ear.

"You left him, man. We don't leave people."

"Really? Where is Tripod?"

"That was different. He was KIA and you know we'll go back for his body. Ike was alive, man. He was alive and you left him like some punk," Indigo shot back.

Salt didn't care. He was alive. The team was alive. The little girl was alive.

"Grim, see if you can get any answers from that little shit."

"Fuck you, coward. Don't give me orders. Indigo is in command."

Indigo rolled his eyes and thought for a moment.

He looked at Grim and then said, "You know they're going to ask when we get there. You may as well try, bro."

Grim nodded and looked down at the little girl sitting between them. She had not moved since they had gotten her back to the vehicle, still wound up in a tight ball.

"Hey, sweetie. Can you tell me your name?" Grim asked.

After a few seconds of not answering, Grim said, "My name is Ronald. I'm a soldier with the US Army. You know, the good guys. Can you tell me your name?"

The little girl started to pick her head up but buried it in her lap again. Grim, forever patient with children thanks to the three daughters he was helping to raise, stayed persistent.

"C'mon, little lady. You can tell me your name. I promise we can get something to eat after. Hell, I'll even take you for ice cream if you can tell me your full name."

The little girl, in her once pretty dress, picked her head up. Her black eyes rolled back in her head as she opened her mouth and hissed. Two fangs grew from her lower gums.

Grim shrieked as she jumped onto his lap like an animal and tore into his neck. The wound was so severe that the sound of his screaming was instantly cut off. Indigo may have been able to react before she attacked him too, but the blood spurting out of Grim's neck had blinded him in his one good eye. He was unable to see anything and was swinging blindly, desperate to feel his fist connect with anything but air.

As Indigo punched at ghosts, the little girl, having had her fill of Grim, abruptly turned and leaped from Grim's lap to the empty front passenger seat. Salt, having barely registered what had been happening, screamed out, more from the surprise scare than the pain, as she ripped his throat out with one swift clinch and tug from her razor-sharp teeth. His scream did not last long either and was replaced with the sound of his exposed artery spurting blood all over the little girl's open, hungry mouth.

Forever the fighter, Indigo managed to get out of the now stopped vehicle and wipe the blood out of his good right eye as the little girl hungrily fed on Salt. Indigo snapped his baton into action and started banging on the LATV. He was taunting and cursing out the little girl with everything he could think of, but she paid no attention to him. She just sat on Salt's lap, licking at the gaping hole in his neck like a thirsty dog at its water bowl.

"Come on, you little cunt, I ain't gonna be your fuckin' dessert," Indigo said, continuing to bang on the vehicle with his baton.

He heard the sound of something rustling behind him and spun, terrified. He was surrounded by the creatures. Based on the bullet holes in their chest, some still oozing that thick, black liquid, Indigo assumed these were the same enemy from back at the church. He shook his head with a chuckle and dropped his baton. With all of the speed he could muster, he pulled his sidearm from its holster. As he raised the handgun, one of the creatures leaped forward and bit down on his wrist. Completely against his will, the gun fell to the ground with a devastating clang. Indigo, now with four of the creatures feeding on him, fell to the ground with only a whimper.

# UNDISCLOSED

# FOURTEEN

**CRAIG SUDDENLY FOUND HIMSELF LICKING** sand off his lips, the grit of the dirt making his already dry tongue feel like the coarsest of sandpaper, removing a layer of skin from his already chapped lips. He looked to his left, to his right, and then realized that he was back in Afghanistan. It was the same nightmare he had every time he closed his eyes. The problem, at least for Craig, was just because you knew you were in a nightmare didn't mean you could change the outcome.

The dreams always started the same way, and no matter how hard he tried, the plan he set in motion would not be changed. The words he spoke, no matter how hard he tried, would be the same words he spoke back then. The dead bodies, the innocent civilians that he was unable to save, would be the same as they were in 2003.

The team had been together for over two years. They were a special operations unit, formed from the best every branch had to offer. Centwally was a sniper from the famed Seal Team Six of the US Navy Seals, Big Lou was a Delta Team member from the US Army, Armando was the best corpsman, or medic, the Marine Corps had to offer, Tim was a Force Recon Marine, and Paul was a demolition expert from the US Army Rangers. All of the men were unmarried, had no kids, were in their late twenties, and had served at least two tours prior to joining the team. Simply put, they were the best professional warriors the United States could put together, which is precisely what made this particular mission so odd.

The team had been tasked with a rather benign mission despite their particular skill set. On this fateful day, they would be patrolling a small hamlet located ten miles south of Bagram Air Base, just west of the Panjshir River. The village had been cleared of all Al-Qaeda and Taliban fighters and had become about as safe as any place could be in an active war zone. While they were more than happy to take on this mundane task, it did make Craig weary as to what they weren't being told. Unfortunately, he was not curious enough to ask any questions.

In the blink of an eye, Craig and his team were driving southbound through the village. They were taking heavy fire from all sides. The sharp *ting* of each bullet striking the vehicle grew louder and louder, each one signifying the weakening armor that was protecting the men. Sitting in the passenger seat of the lead vehicle, Craig had identified and eliminated two men, each one tucked inside small alleyways that served more as a ground-level sewer system. Seeing the pattern, Craig began to advise the team to focus fire on the alleys when he and Tim, who was driving the lead LATV, noticed a massive problem through the bullet-scarred windshield.

The main road in the village had an east-to-west cross-section at the halfway point through town. This divide seemed to be designed with the intention of keeping the living quarters of the villagers separate from the town's open-air market on the southwest end. The north side, both east and west had tiny clay huts, separated by scattered alleys with the entire east side of the village covered in lush poppy fields.

Moving toward the team from south to west was a ten-man enemy fire team. They were calmly walking down the road, concentrating all of their fire on the lead vehicle. Craig and Tim understood that they were going to die shortly before they noticed that most of the enemy fire was missing them wide on their left. Tim was smiling, almost relaxing from the knowledge that these amateurs had no chance if this was the best they had. Craig, less apt to hubris, saw the large pile of trash on the northwest side of the crossroad. The enemy combatants were not missing them, they were steering them right into the pile of trash. In this particular part of the world, that meant only one thing—an improvised explosive device.

Tim noticed the IED just in time and swerved hard left in order to avoid any contact. The enemy advance had stopped on the south end of the crossroad. They were laying down heavy fire, absolutely beginning to turn the LATV into Swiss cheese. The hard left turn Tim had made would have normally taken the team down the east side of the village's main crossroad, but the insurgents set up a heavy barbed wire barricade. A lesser wheelman would have gotten the vehicle stuck or tried to ram it. Tim, being one of the best in the world, was not traveling fast enough to make such a foolish mistake. Due to his ability to maintain a slow and constant speed, the U-turn performed was about as perfect as any driver's ed teacher could hope for... also making it easier for the second LATV to follow suit.

The rifle fire that had been coming from the alleys when the team first entered the village had slowed down since most of the combatants were dead. Craig was about to take the opportunity to radio back the ambush to Bagram but heard an explosion behind him, followed immediately by the rear tires of the LATV lifting off the ground. Tim was able to maintain control of the vehicle despite the flat rear right tire. If the road they were traveling on had not been paved, they would have been stuck and dead.

"Vehicle two is down!" Big Lou shouted from the backseat.

The LATV came to an abrupt stop. Big Lou and Tim's doors flew open in unison, and they began to lay down suppressing fire. Craig, upon exiting the vehicle, made his way to the crash site, concentrating on getting to his downed men rather than firing on the enemy. Before he had even reached the overturned vehicle, Armando had made his way out of the backseat and was starting to triage Centwally and Paul's wounds. Seeing that Armando had the medical side taken care of, Craig began to join Tim and Big Lou in laying down covering fire.

With only minor wounds being reported, Armando was able to transport both Centwally and Paul from the crashed vehicle and was loading them into the back of LATV One when it became clear they were far too heavy to make it out of the village on the flat tire.

Tim took his position behind the steering wheel. Armando, after getting Centwally and Paul into the back seat, was ordered into the front passenger seat by Craig. Big Lou had taken up residence in the turret on the roof that housed the mounted .50 caliber machine gun. Still taking heavy fire from the remaining Taliban fighters, Craig, who had been hanging onto the passenger side door, jumped off of the LATV. As he did, the heavily armored vehicle lurched forward and began to slowly roll northbound. Craig jogged alongside the vehicle, and although the pings and zips from rounds just missing him was enough to keep him moving, he could feel himself slowing down. The rest of the team was returning fire, doing their best to cover him, but the addition of three men, two wounded did not make for great combat effectiveness. How effective could you be if you could not move more than three to five degrees left to right?

"C'mon, you old bastard. Push it!" Craig heard one of the guys say as he felt a sharp, burning sting in his right hip.

His initial thought, for whatever reason, was he should have drunk more water. As he flew off his feet and landed face down on the hard, hot road, he thought to himself: *More water? You were shot, dickhead.*

The LATV stopped, but Craig shouted for them to keep going without him. He could see the vehicle shift from left to right as the guys tried to free up enough room to exit but were too cramped. Once again, he shouted for them to leave. The boys, or at least Tim, finally seemed to get the hint and slowly began to drive the damaged vehicle out of the village.

Due to the thick smoke from the IED that crippled vehicle two, Craig had a small bit of cover as he crawled to the west side of the road. The east side, while also having seven clay and straw-built homes, did not have the luxury of the alleyways, the hospital that had been blown to shit a year prior, or the equally destroyed former government building. Any of these would have provided sufficient cover for days. Essentially, he had no place to really hide on the east side of the village. Craig knew the west side of the village, specifically the northwest side, had the best places to hunker down and wait for the cavalry. After all, he only had two magazines left for his M4, his sidearm with an extra clip, and his knife. The team, he estimated, would be back to Bagram in twenty minutes. The rapid response team would take ten minutes to get rolling and another ten to fifteen to extract him, assuming they came in with choppers, guns a-blazing. Craig made his way into an empty home where he was able to prop himself up against the front door, laying on his left side. Craig removed his belt, unbuttoned his button, and unzipped his pants. He stuck the dirty cloth belt, double folded it into his mouth, and began to pull down his pants. The pain was unrelenting as he methodically slid his trousers down an inch at a time, first the left side and then the right, until the wound in his hip was exposed. As he caught his breath and tried to slow his heart rate, he spit out the belt. It apparently did its job as nobody had yet to burst in and put two rounds in the back of his skull.

A quick inspection of the wound found while it was deep, the bullet had not stuck. Really, it was a graze... just incredibly deep. But, with no medical supplies, his options were limited, and he slid himself, still cognizant of the noise he was making, to the fire, burning crisply in the corner of the one-room home. He drew his knife and laid it in the fire. As he waited for the blade to get hot enough, he quietly allowed himself to chuckle at the thought of a Taliban fighter walking into this hut right now. He would find Craig laying in front of a fire with bare ass hanging out and blood steadily pouring off the top of his hip, like a chocolate fountain you'd see at a bougie wedding.

*Eat your heart out, ladies,* he thought to himself, resting his hand just above his hip with his elbow cocked at a ninety-degree angle like he was posing for a photograph.

Satisfied that the knife was sterile enough, Craig put his old friend, the belt, back into his mouth and drew the knife out of the fire. The searing red hot blade made Craig rethink this plan, but one look at his hip told him this was his only option. He took three deep breaths in quick succession and laid the blade over the bullet wound in his right hip. The pain mixed with the smell of his searing flesh was enough to make him start to lose consciousness... stranded... during a war... behind enemy lines... in Afghanistan. The word fucked can be used in so many ways. Craig deemed its use as a verb was best for his current situation. He was fucked.

# FIFTEEN

**IT TOOK EVERY BIT OF** sixty seconds for Craig to make his way back to reality. Confused, he looked around the room quickly, attempting to get his bearings. He was no longer in Afghanistan but wasn't at home either. This was not his living room, his recliner, tv, or carpet. Then he started to remember. He was in Helm's Hamlet, Iowa. Population: Zero. Well, one resident, if you counted him, but he had no intention of staying. He had been tasked with a mission.

Then, it all came back to him. Every last second of this miserable day. Despite everything, the shame of needing to sleep for the last hour was the worst thought in his mind.

Craig rose from his reclining chair and stretched his arms out, pushing the limits of the tendons in his shoulders and rolled his neck from right to left. The cracking confirmed what he already knew: he was past his expiration date. He took a deep breath and decided he needed to see if anything was happening outside. Although he had been dreading it since he had been startled awake, Craig had to say the words out loud, as if that were the only way he could believe it himself.

"Any fucking monsters out there?"

He peered out the window, wishing for the good old days of Afghanistan. *The dust storms, the lack of water, the human enemies that died when shot. The good old days indeed.* Craig almost turned the old man's reading lamp off to get a better look at Main Street and to better conceal himself, but something told him not to. Something from earlier in the day kept nagging him that the light was his best friend right now, although he couldn't figure out why.

Hardly the most important part of the cluster fuck he found himself embroiled in, Craig stopped worrying about the lamp and focused on the new mission: getting the fuck out of this town. He scanned right and left across Main Street, pausing for a few seconds each time in order to take in every last detail. Craig looked for potholes, cracks in the asphalt, debris, or anything that could hinder his escape. And, of course, the creatures. As stupid as it felt, he found it helpful to say the word out loud.

"Monsters."

Seeing all he would be able to from this limited vantage point, Craig had two real choices left. He could get up to the roof where he would have a complete three-hundred-and-sixty-degree view of the town. This would give him a better idea of not only how to get out of this place but also let him look for signs of survivors. The downside to this plan? There could be creatures on the roof looking for him, he could expose his whereabouts to the monsters, or he may be unable to get down if compromised.

The second plan was not as elegant. He'd simply walk right out the front door. Again, this was not an elegant plan. Craig checked the small amount of ammunition he had: the M11 had one full magazine left on top of the one round he had chambered. While most intelligent, tactical, and seasoned operatives would have chosen plan one, Craig was sick and tired of waiting around. His tactical prowess thus far had netted him exactly jack shit. He went into the old man's kitchen and turned on the cold-water tap. As the water started to pour out, Craig put his mouth under the stream and drank. Satisfied, he turned the water off, wiped his mouth on his sleeve, and exited the old man's apartment, closing the door quietly.

He eased his way down the stairs and felt his way through the pitch-black store, banging into a shelf or promotional stand in the aisle every few feet. Once he had reached the front door, he stopped for a brief moment and listened. He closed his eyes and heard nothing but crickets. The glow from the fire at the crash site was like a beacon for him. All he had to do was make it to that fire, turn right, and he would find himself on the road the team had used to come into town. His only hope was that he didn't cross paths with any more of these creatures.

All signs pointing to the coast being clear, Craig unlocked the door, opened it, and started sprinting down Main Street with everything he had. The feeling like something was nipping at his heels made the pain in his hip almost nonexistent as he pushed himself to run faster. *Just keep running,* he thought to himself. Every time he thought his lungs would burst, his heart would explode, or his left leg would simply just fall off, he swore he could smell the copper smell of blood from a creature's mouth closing in on him. He could hear the snapping of teeth behind him and the breeze it caused on his neck. Craig would find another gear and run harder every time that happened. He felt like one of these creatures was just playing with him. Maybe even forcing him into an ambush, like Afghanistan.

As he reached the beginning of the field where the crashed plane was still burning, Craig decided that something was in fact running right behind him. Ambush or not, he was sick of this shit. Sick of the running, sick of being scared, sick of being ignorant, underprepared, and set up. The anger welling up inside of him now was starting to cloud his judgment. He knew this was stupid. He just didn't care. Every person has their breaking point. That moment when facing your fear becomes more palatable than living another second in fear.

About three yards into the corn, Craig pulled the M11 from its holster, steadfast in the plan and the gun firmly locked into his right hand, index finger on the trigger, he was ready. His right thumb flipped the safety off, and in one fluid motion, Craig used the momentum of his sprinting to catapult himself forward. As he did, he rotated his body, midair, one hundred eighty degrees. The fall from landing on his back did its job as the force of the impact caused his index finger to reflexively depress the trigger. The handgun began to crack the almost silent night like a sudden thunderstorm.

The first round struck the airborne creature in the throat, a loud hiss became a gurgle as black liquid poured from the creature's voice box. The rest of the magazine, all fourteen rounds, entered the body in an almost perfect line down the center of the creature. It had attempted to pounce on Craig, but the force of the bullets entering the body stopped it midair, causing the creature to crumble to the ground in a heap. Not waiting for the inevitable jump scare that comes at the end of every scary movie, Craig removed the now empty magazine and let it fall to the ground. He drew the last mag for his M11, reloaded the weapon, chambered a round, and then put two rounds in the back of the creature's skull. Craig paused a moment, letting the ringing in his ears cease, then listened for any further movement. Satisfied, he holstered his sidearm and once again took out his knife. Imagining that this creature was Agent Smith, sitting comfortably back at base, he began to saw back and forth at the monster's neck.

Satisfied with his second confirmed kill, Craig made his way to the road with a new sense of pride. When he found a LATV with three of its doors open, the driver's side door being the only one closed, he truly thought his luck was starting to change. As he approached, he saw there were two bodies, one in the driver's seat and one in the seat behind the driver. It was only when he was standing over them that he realized he knew these men.

Although he had desperately wanted to kill them himself, Craig had to admit that the Dark River guys probably didn't deserve to go out like this. Craig looked over the bodies and took personal items: dog tags, letters to loved ones, the wedding rings for their families. They would almost certainly never know how their loved ones died. Craig figured, for once, that was probably for the best. The least he could do was return whatever personal effects these men had to their families. It was the unwritten code.

He pulled the almost decapitated body of Salt out of the driver's seat and placed him in the back seat with Grimm. There was a bloody lump lying in the middle of the road that had once been Indigo. His body was so ravaged and torn to pieces that there was nothing Craig could do to get a significant part of him into the vehicle. He would have to leave the mass that used to be Indigo in the street. This made all of the pride and luck he was feeling disappear. He told himself he didn't have time to feel shame just yet and suddenly remembered that there had been a fourth passenger. Craig looked around quickly for the girl in the immediate area but could find no sign of her. He climbed into the driver's seat and turned the engine over. With a passenger load of the two mutilated and partially devoured bodies of Salt and Grimm, he headed back for base. Had he been paying more attention, not allowing his emotions to dampen his focus, Craig would have noticed the set of eyes watching him from the dark.

# SIXTEEN

## SPECIAL OPS

**TYPICALLY, THE SECURITY AROUND A** forward operating base was insanely tight. Nothing could deter a military operation from going tits up like a security breach on base. The security as Craig approached the base was lax to say the least. As a matter of fact, it was perfectly clear that this base was being shut down, posthaste. Craig drove the LATV past the abandoned checkpoint, pressing the gas pedal a bit harder, hoping he had the opportunity to thank whoever was responsible for everything that had happened since he had arrived. The lies, the abandonment, the team that left him to die. Someone had to answer for this, and he had his mind made up as to who that someone was going to be.

The vehicle came to a complete stop outside of the main control center for the makeshift base. The uniformed personnel that had been running back and forth had all but disappeared. Most of the equipment, once making the entire room buzz, had been shut down; a few consoles completely torn out of their mounting. Craig glanced around for anyone that looked like they could help him. Finally, he heard the faint sound of bickering voices from around the area where the team had first been briefed. As he got closer, he could tell the voices belonged to Agent Smith and General Andrews.

Craig approached the area and listened quietly as the two argued over the failed operation. The general was confident that the team would resurface, but Smith was happy to call this a tie, the weaponized fungi they recovered was a win. The loss of the team, the town, and "that Eve bitch" being the only downside. Too pissed off to think as clearly as he should have, Craig burst into the briefing area as Smith and General Andrews both gasped and recoiled backward. Agent Smith was in total shock. General Andrews, the seasoned military man, was falling back in order to buy himself an extra second to comprehend what was happening.

Smith, finally realizing that the intruder was Craig, began to relax his posture. This was his first major mistake. Just as he let his right hand ease away from his sidearm, the smile on his face began to spread. Smith opened his mouth to speak, but Craig's thick left hand was squeezing his throat, making speech a dubious proposition at best. The agent instinctively began tapping on the arm of his assailant, signaling he was "tapping out" or giving up. Craig didn't care. With a heavy growl, Craig lifted him and performed, what wrestling aficionados would call, a chokeslam onto the briefing table. Craig eased off of Smith's throat just enough for the CIA agent to find the breath that the impact of the table took from him. As his eyes filled with water, due to fear more than pain, Smith saw his imminent death as Craig drew his sidearm and stuck it against Smith's temple.

"Take it easy, Ike," Andrews said cautiously as he slowly raised his arms, subliminally telling Craig to calm down.

"Was it his decision or yours?" Craig asked, not taking his eyes off Smith.

"Ike, you know how these things go."

Craig pulled the hammer back on his pistol, pressing it harder against Smith's temple.

General Andrews took a deep breath and tried again. "It doesn't matter who made the decision, Craig. We were both in the room."

Craig nodded his head slowly and began to loosen his grip on Smith's throat as he steadily pulled the gun away from his head. Smith caught his breath quickly and had a bit of drool spilling out of the right side of his mouth.

"God damn, psycho! I fucking scrubbed your mission. You're done, you has-been. You..."

Smith never got the rest of the sentence out as he was interrupted by the sound of Craig's pistol. The ringing in his ears distracted Smith for a little over a second before he noticed the trail of smoke. Smith followed the tiny trail of smoke to its source and realized he had been shot in the leg. He began to scream as the room quickly filled with armed men and women in uniform, having heard the shot, all pointing their primary weapons at Craig.

"You're lucky I only left you with a limp, you piece of shit!"

"Stand down!" General Andrews shouted, breaking through the screams of the newly hobbled Agent Smith.

Craig was unsure who the general was speaking to, so he let his gun fall to the ground and raised his hands high in the air, signaling his surrender. Craig saw the rest of the people who had suddenly filled the room also lower their weapons.

"Someone get him to the medical tent," General Andrews ordered.

"He's gonna need a hospital, I'm afraid," Craig said sarcastically.

"Shut up, you idiot!" Andrews shouted.

Craig did as he was ordered as the now sobbing Smith was being escorted out of the room. Two privates with military police patches handcuffed Craig, and he was ordered to be detained in the brig.

There were, no matter where you were in life, certainties. In this case, a forward operating base would certainly always house a mess area, a weapons depot, and a brig. The brig was a bit like a detention center but one where the guards simply didn't give a shit enough to check on you. Once you were locked away on one of these bases, you may as well have been lost in the Bermuda Triangle. Craig felt the alone time would be nice, given the day he'd just had. He was also confident they would either be ready to push off in an hour or they would need to go back into Helm's Hamlet. Either way, he knew better than to get comfortable.

As he was being led away, Craig said, "General, I brought back two bodies, both KIA. Two more KIAs need to be recovered. You know what we're facing back in Helm's Hamlet. You know where to find me when you're ready to debrief me."

"Get him the fuck out of here," Andrews said, trying to keep his voice steady and pointing toward the door.

"Oh, I also found at least one survivor. Possibly some more in town. If these things are what I think, we got sunrise in three hours. Daylight would be a great time to sweep the town."

General Andrews considered this for a few moments as Craig was escorted out of the room. He looked around the room and angrily pointed at a corporal and a specialist.

"Corporal, get the remains out of that LATV. Specialist, tell Lieutenant Bradwell to notify Dark River of their loss. Everyone else, get back to work."

Confident he had the room to himself, General Andrews picked up the phone in the middle of the table.

"Yeah, this is Andrews. I need Ronda Alexander out of Springfield and all files relating to Project Speartip."

Not waiting for an answer to his order, he hung up the phone and fell back into his chair. He shook his head as he removed his cap and rubbed his scalp. Andrews whistled in amazement as he looked at Smith's blood on the floor and chuckled.

"Somebody get me some God damned coffee!"

# SEVENTEEN

**THE HELICOPTER WAS ABOUT TWENTY** feet from landing on the ground when the door flung open. As the chopper lowered itself to Earth, General Andrews could see the answer to all his problems staring back at him with a smile and a nod as if to say: Yes, I am the answer to your problems, and yes, you may breathe easy again.

Ten feet from the ground and the general saw the woman in the back of the helicopter unbuckling her seat belt. He chuckled and shook his head. The wind created by the landing helicopter forced the general to place his right hand over his cap and duck his head, trying to keep the dust from invading his eyes.

When he heard the bird taking off again, he lifted his head to see her standing right in front of him.

"Sleeping on the job, General?" She asked. Her voice was raspy from years of chain-smoking during operations.

"Do you ever stop busting balls, Agent Alexander?"

"No. I suppose that's why I'm in this fucking state instead of having dinner with the President tonight," she said with a smile.

General Andrews never understood how a five-foot-two-inch woman could command every room she entered, but she did. If Craig was the military's best soldier, Ronda Alexander was the best intelligence officer in the game. She was smart, tenacious, unapologetic, and completely unable to play company politics.

Andrews was so captivated that he did not notice the equally diminutive woman standing behind Ronda.

With a tilt of his head, Andrews smiled and stuck out his hand, "And you are?"

"Look at me, a man in uniform stands before me and I lose all track of polite behavior," Ronda started, laughing at her own lame joke.

"General Robert Andrews, this is Special Agent Katherine Rigol."

"You can call me Katy, General," the brown-haired, twenty-something-year-old woman said with a tight smile and firm handshake.

"A pleasure," Andrews turned his attention back to Ronda. "Have you read up on what we're dealing with?"

"You mean the plagues or Craig Eitel?"

"Yes," General Andrews replied, an attempt at levity.

Katy chuckled. Ronda did not.

"Well, let's go discuss which one is worse," Ronda said, extending her right arm and motioning for the general to lead the way to a place they could talk.

Before Ronda followed the general, she advised Katy to look around and get to know the area. What that really meant was to sweep the base for any suspicious activity, find the weapons cache and restock it with the "tools" that were being flown right behind the ladies. By the time Ronda and Andrews had finished speaking, Katy had discovered rumblings of monsters in the cornfields, a few privates wanting to go AWOL, she had accounted for and stored the new weapons, and she had discovered the prisoner was fairly wary of representatives of the Central Intelligence Agency. Satisfied, Ronda asked for Craig to be brought into the briefing room.

# EIGHTEEN

**"HIYA THERE," RONDA GREETED CRAIG** as he was escorted into the room in handcuffs and ankle cuffs connected by a chain.

"Hiiiii," Katy said with a rolling wave of her fingers, her legs kicked up on the briefing table.

If this was meant to disarm Craig, he was impressed with how well it had worked.

"Um, hello, ladies."

Ronda, not looking up from the file she was holding, asked the MPs escorting Craig to sit him down in the chair across the table from the two women. Once seated, Ronda dismissed the MPs. They turned on a dime and obediently exited the room. Craig assumed this tactic was to show how tough the ladies were or, at the very least, how unintimidated they were by Craig. Turns out, neither was true. Ronda just wanted to speak privately.

"So, Craig. Let's get to the point. How fucked up are you?"

"I don't believe I am, ma'am."

"Cut the 'ma'am' shit, Craig. My name is Ronda. For the record, you are very fucked up. You should hear the way this report reads. It's terrifying. You just came back from a vigilante mission on US soil. You wiped out a small town in the heartland of the very country you swore an oath to protect. The rest of your paramilitary organization was taken out. Your defense is that the town became overrun with monsters... not figurative but literal monsters. Sounds to me like you are batshit crazy."

Katy leaned in and whispered something to Ronda. Ronda looked at her confused for a moment but resigned herself to believing whatever Katy had said, nodding her head solemnly.

"Apparently, batshit crazy is a derogatory term we don't use anymore. You have some very serious mental health issues, Mr. Eitel."

Craig became very aware of what was happening halfway through her story. He was being set up as the patsy, which he should have expected, but he was so blinded by rage that putting a bullet in Smith was a need, not a want. Trying to prevent that from happening was an impossibility. *Maybe prison could help me with my anger issues*, he thought.

"Yeah, you got me pegged, in more ways than one, it seems."

Katy burst out in a genuine, hearty laugh. Ronda smirked and looked up from the file she had been reading for the first time since Craig entered the room. Craig took the moment of levity to skip any more of the games that were so often played in these situations. He had to ask.

"So, can you start to tell me exactly what you want from me? Do we all have to sit through the 'deal' I can make with you and how lucky I am to have you in my corner?"

"What did I tell you, Katy? This is our guy. Am I right?"

Katy didn't take her eyes off of Craig but nodded and squinted at him. Craig attempted to look as nonplussed as possible. Inside though, he did not like the feeling of this young lady staring into his soul. He thought he had seen some dead eye killers before, but this woman was different.

Ronda, still smirking, said, "Okay, Craig, I would like to skip over the games too. I'm very happy you understand the score. Here's the skinny. General Andrews and almost everyone involved in this little fuck up would like to drop a MOAB on the town, declare some sort of accident and call it a day. They already have the town memorial ribbons design prepared and the phony charity drive for the 'survivors.' Are you with me so far?"

Craig could not believe MOABs were in play—the mother of all bombs, or MOAB, was the largest, non-nuclear, explosive device the US military had. It essentially had all of the physical and raw power of a nuclear bomb minus the radiation. You could technically drop one of these bad boys and be at the impact sight the next day enjoying your new wasteland. Whoever was even thinking of this as a viable option was not privy to any of the intelligence Craig had.

"Ma'am, I mean, Ronda. There are survivors in Helm's Hamlet. Citizens. We can't drop a bomb on them. We absolutely can't drop *these* bombs on them."

"Our data shows that ninety-two percent of the homes in Helm's Hamlet have a basement or storm cellar they could take shelter in. If they are still alive, they have probably been there since yesterday anyway. If they stay still, they should be able to survive the blasts," Katy said, speaking up for the first time.

"No. That's more collateral damage justification bullshit. I won't do this anymore. Give me a team. Give me a real briefing. Give me all the guns you got. I'll bring you every survivor left in that town.

Ronda gave Craig a wink and a finger gun with her right hand just before saying to him, "I was hoping you'd say that. I already have your team on the way."

"Really? Are they more reliable than the fuckers who just ditched me?"

"How would I know? They're your team."

"What? I haven't even met th—" he started before the words got stuck in his throat.

Ronda looked at Katy amused, "I think he gets it now."

Craig looked at her like she had just punched his mother in the face. *What kind of game was this lady playing? Was she just psychotic?*

"You mean my team? Like, literally my team. My guys?"

"You got it, tiger."

"That would be a colossal mistake on your part."

"You know, that's exactly what your team said too. Like I told them, you'll soon come to find that I simply do not give a fuck. Now, let's get you properly briefed. Well, after you get cleaned up, of course."

CRAIG WAS ESCORTED, BY KATY, out of the briefing room and into a makeshift decontamination tent. He assumed that this was here just in case the zombie virus had become active. Regardless, Craig appreciated the scalding hot shower, fresh towel, and his new clothes. He dressed quickly, laced up his boots, and felt like a new man.

"Looking like a warrior," Katy said with a grin after Craig had emerged from the tent.

"Feeling like a warrior, ma'am."

"C'mon, tough guy. Ronda is waiting for us," Katy said as she began walking back to the main briefing room.

The thoughts going through Craig's mind were like a tornado. His team being called back into action was enough to push him over the edge alone. It had been a few years since any of them spoke to him. He wrote and called to no avail. He could hardly blame them, though. What happened ruined everything for them. Craig lost his job, but they lost their families, jobs, friends, and freedom. Largely because of him.

That reunion would take place soon enough. Right now, however, Craig was more concerned with this briefing he was supposed to receive. The last briefing led to four casualties and a new limp for Vernon Smith. If he was not made fully aware of this upcoming mission, he knew nobody would be coming home.

It suddenly dawned on him, and then all his concerns seemed to evaporate. He didn't work for anyone here. He was employed by AAA Security, based out of Columbus, Ohio. He was a mall security guard. If anything in this briefing even smelled a bit fishy to him, he would simply leave. Sure, they could arrest or kill him for everything he knew, not to mention for what he had done to Agent Smith, but that was a chance he was willing to take. Dead by two slugs in the back of the head or in jail for life, it definitely beats being torn apart by whatever those things were. For the first time in a long time, Craig felt as though he held all the cards, even if he were lying to himself.

The briefing room was hardly the spectacle it was when Craig first arrived. The staff that had been running around with such furious purpose were gone. The only people in the entire room other than him were General Andrews, Special Agent in Charge Ronda Alexander, and Field Agent Katy Rigol. The room had a somber and ominous feeling to it. The circus was gone. This was all business.

"Take a seat, Craig," General Andrews said angrily.

"Yes, sir," Craig said in reply and sat down in the seat Andrews pointed to.

He had every right to be pissed at him, Craig knew, but these were not the type of men that had those conversations. They may never go back to the relationship they once had. Deep down, Craig was fine with that too.

"Mr. Eitel," Ronda started, "How much do you know about Kola Superdeep Borehole?"

"Well, that would be absolutely nothing."

"Then strap in. This is going to be a bit long."

Ronda took a long drink from the glass of water that had been sitting next to her. A deep breath and a long exhale later, Ronda began her briefing.

# TWENTY

## REDACTED

**"IT WAS 1970 WHEN THE** USSR began to drill what is now known as the Kola Superdeep Borehole. The space race had been lost, and the Communist government of the former Soviet Union needed a new 'patriotic' endeavor. Documents, only available now, show some of those in the upper echelon of Brezhnev's cabinet wondered how exactly this was going to dwarf the United States' Apollo missions to the moon. The answers, the few on record, were unsatisfactory.

"Never try to get inside the mind of a Communist," Katy said with a chuckle.

"What we do know is that the Soviets drilled into the Earth for nineteen years, finally stopping in 1989. The accepted reason as to why the project was halted was fairly obvious. The triumph of capitalism had thrown the once steadfast Russian people into chaos. Those who had suffered under the tyrannical guise of the 'people's government' now had more important things to worry about than a twelve-thousand-meter hole that had since yielded no tangible scientific uses."

Craig asked, "So, essentially, it was just a big hole."

"Exactly, according to public record."

"Okay, I'll bite. What did the classified report say?"

"They stopped because they found something. The fall of the USSR was a convenient excuse for all parties involved."

"All parties?"

"Yes, Craig, all parties. The Soviets, the Chinese, and us."

"Okay, this just doesn't make sense. You just named three countries that all hate one another. Why would all three of us be working together? What did they find?"

"They found the canister you retrieved for us today."

Craig was flabbergasted. He just sat there with his mouth agape. Ronda took his silence as an opportunity to continue her briefing.

"There is a far lesser-known superdeep borehole on a ranch in the Southwestern United States. Although the US had won the space race, they were not about to concede any ground right when the Cold War had started to get a lot warmer. The threat of nuclear war was pounded into the psyche of both countries' citizens, and the US was in the early stages of the most unpopular ground war in American history. All in the name of stopping the 'red scare.'"

Ronda paused before continuing, "While they knew it would more than likely lead to absolutely nothing, funding was approved for the United States to begin drilling its very own borehole. The mission was simple, go exactly one foot deeper than our intel told us the Russians could go."

"And?" Craig asked impatiently.

"We made it within one hundred meters of the Russians, and then we found something too."

"Let me guess, a seven to eight-foot sarcophagus?"

Ronda chuckled a bit before saying, "No, don't be ridiculous. We found another biological agent inside a metallic silver canister. Unfortunately, there was no practical use for it, so the canister and its contents were incinerated. Which reminds me, your team did a fine job recovering the Zombie Virus. Before you ask, it is currently en route to one of our facilities... and yes, it is also going to be destroyed."

Undeterred by her empty compliments, Craig asked, "So where did the coffin come from?"

"Well... the Chinese found the coffin, of course. When they were approximately two/thirds of the way to matching Russia's depth."

# TWENTY ONE

**WHILE CRAIG WAS BEING BRIEFED** just outside of Helm's Hamlet, Iowa, a large helicopter was landing 324 miles away at the federal prison located in Leavenworth, Kansas. The transport was to fly the five prisoners twenty minutes to Kansas City's private airstrip, and from there, they would catch the same Learjet that Craig had taken a day earlier to the base in Iowa. If all went to plan, they would be reunited with their team lead in just under two hours.

When the men had arrived at the prison a few years ago, they were wearing orange jumpsuits, shackled from wrist to ankle, and issued a seven-digit prisoner identification number. If you had ever wondered how quickly you could strip a human being of their dignity, the answer was easy. Reduce their entire being to seven digits. Leaving the prison today, you never would have guessed these men had served one day in prison. They were freshly shaven, with brand new haircuts. They were issued all-black fatigues and black military-style boots. The feeling each one of them had quietly thought they would never feel again came rushing back as they marched single file to the helicopter. It felt like pride.

The twenty-two-minute flight to Kansas City would have been awkward save for the loud rotating blades and air passing over the chopper that had mercifully made the situation too loud for casual conversation. The team had not seen one another since they had arrived in prison eighteen months ago. For security reasons, they would have preferred the team be transferred to five different facilities, but it became evident after a few months of trying that this group had no real desire to be around one another anyway. The warden and prison board agreed that these prisoners had been broken. What they didn't realize was these men weren't broken by the prison system. They had been broken the day they were betrayed by the very life they had saved. Had they let Craig die, they would still be free men.

Once they had boarded their private aircraft, taken their seats, and jet took off, the boys started to loosen up around each other. The cold stares and frustrated exhales were replaced by a few nods and fist bumps. Ten minutes into their sixty-minute flight, Armando could no longer stand the awkwardness in the cabin of the seven-seater aircraft.

"So, you guys all look like shit."

Everyone laughed except for Paul. He didn't care if the best comedian ever started performing their stand-up comedy routine. He was not laughing. The thought of having to work with Craig again, let alone working for him, made him sick to his stomach. The rest of the guys may forgive and forget but not Paul DiBernardo. If holding a grudge was a person, it would be Paul. The last time this team had been together in a combat situation had catastrophic results that had cost Paul not only his freedom but his wife and kid. As far as he was concerned, Craig was responsible for that.

"Can you guys believe this shit is really happening?" Lou asked, sounding more concerned than curious.

"Hell yes, I believe it. I knew that when it got bad enough, they would dust us off and put us to work," Tim replied.

"They aren't using us because we're the best. They're using us because we are already dead to them. We're the fucking definition of expendable," Paul said, immediately sucking the fun out of this mini reunion.

"So why are you here," Armando asked, a bit more hostile sounding than he had intended.

"I'm here to kill Ike. Why are you here?"

# CLASSIFIED

# TWENTY TWO

**"WE STILL HAVE A LOT** to discuss—" Craig started to say from his seat in the briefing room.

"We'll do your after-action report when the team arrives. At which time we will go over everything in detail," Ronda interrupted.

"This better be better than your last briefing. All I know now is the history of this shit, and even that was pretty vague."

Ronda rolled her eyes and let out an exasperated breath before she said, "I shared information with you that I didn't have to. I did so in order to demonstrate to you that I am a team player, unlike Agent Smith. It was a courtesy."

Craig just nodded his head. He knew she was correct. It seemed to Craig that Ronda was probably not wrong all that often. Everything about her exuded confidence and power, but her overall demeanor was light, almost conversational. She was the type of person you could have a beer with or plan a political assassination to perfection.

"That's fair, I suppose. Let's stick with the history in that case. Why was the United States harboring these biological weapons? How did they get buried that deep? How long had they been down there? Where were you transporting them to? Why did the plane crash?" Craig asked, his speech picking up speed with every question he asked.

"Slow down, old man. You're gonna have a heart attack," Katy laughed.

"Craig, don't ask questions. Take the information you're given and follow your orders," General Andrews snapped at him.

"I no longer work for you, General Andrews. All due respect, get over Smith and stay out of my way," Craig uncharacteristically snapped back.

"Okay, boys. Let's call this one a tie, huh?" Ronda asked rhetorically.

Both men were ready to start throwing fists before she started talking. They knew who was in charge in this room. The way they both shut up, it was clear that it was neither of them.

"Ma'am," Craig started, focusing his attention back on Ronda, "I am happy to help, and frankly, you need me out there."

"I agree."

"Good, then I would like to make it very clear that I am a civilian. I am not employed by the United States military or any government agency. I'm here of my own free will and can leave anytime I see fit."

Ronda, Katy, and even Andrews started laughing hysterically, much to his dismay. He had never stood up for himself against the brass and now was feeling foolish for doing so. He felt like a child who had tested his parents' limits. Rather than taking him seriously, they were looking at him as a fool.

"Did you practice that speech much before you delivered it?" Ronda asked.

"Oh, yeah, he definitely was rehearsing that," Katy added sarcastically.

Craig could feel his face getting hot from the embarrassment. He wanted to get mad but found himself as humble as he was confused. *Was he wrong? He was just a guy now. What leverage did they have?*

"Craig, we need to clear this up once and for all. You can leave, but I know you won't... and so do you."

"How do you know?"

"Because I know you. You're a junkie. Your drug is an enemy to hunt and kill. You also have a chance to rewrite your own history. But if I'm wrong, you know where the door is."

Craig knew she was right, again. He would never walk out on this mission, but her last comment had got the wheels in his head turning. Agent Alexander had him dead to rights, but he had one last ace up his sleeve. If he couldn't get out of this, maybe then he could get something out of it.

"You're probably right," Craig said, "but you're going to need to pony up on your end. I want something."

"I've been fairly transparent with you, Mr. Eitel. That should be enough."

"It's not. You're being forthright because it suits your needs right now. I want full pardons for every member of my team. They will never spend another day in prison."

Ronda thought about that earnestly for a moment. Everyone else at the table sat in silence as they watched the person in charge debate the variables.

"You have a deal, Craig, with one exception."

Satisfied, Craig smirked as he asked, "What exception?"

"Everyone receives a pardon if you can complete your objective. The job gets done, or you don't come home. If you retreat, everyone burns."

"Fair enough. What exactly is our objective?"

Ronda thought for a moment and said, "We'll save that for the full team brief."

"Okay, what should we talk about in that case? Did you guys want to play a board game or something while we wait?" Craig asked, looking around at everyone in the room.

"I'd like you to brief us, Craig," Ronda said, unfazed by his attempt at humor.

"My after-action report should definitely wait until the rest of the boys are here. They should hear firsthand what I experienced in that fucking town."

Ronda nodded her head with her face twisted in a way that spoke to Craig with no words necessary. She was saying: *no shit, asshole.*

"I agree, Mr. Eitel. What I had in mind is just for us. I want to hear from you about what happened in Afghanistan and the subsequent court martial. I'd also like to hear from you in your own words what the men on this team were like. I only spoke to them for five minutes. So, speak."

# SECRET CONTENTS

# TWENTY

# THREE

**AS ORDERED, CRAIG BEGAN TO** speak. He described that fateful day in Afghanistan with as many details as he could deliver. He went over the heat, the wind beating them with tiny grains of sand, and the strangeness of his team taking a routine patrol in what was supposed to be an already cleared and friendly village. The rest of the group stayed silent as Craig exhaustively itemized each and every move the team made once the firefight had started. He thought for a second he would get some sort of audible response from someone in the peanut gallery, but instead, they continued to listen to his story, stone-faced. After he described being shot in the hip and crawling into a small clay hut for cover, he had to pause. This is where the nightmare for him always stopped. It had never dawned on Craig until just now that he had never had to relive the rest of that day since the trial.

Craig swallowed hard before continuing his story.

"After I was in the hut, I had to cauterize the wound using the fire inside to sterilize my knife and passed out for a few minutes. I woke up to a hand touching my mouth. I still had my knife in hand and immediately pushed it into my would-be attacker's sternum. Fully cognizant a moment later, I realized I had stabbed a boy—maybe twelve or thirteen. I quickly looked for some sort of weapon that would at least justify my actions at the time, but there was nothing."

He had been looking down at his fidgeting hands while telling this part of the story, trying to hide his shame. Everyone was looking at him, but there was no judgment in their eyes. The three other people around this table had to commit terrible acts in the name of their country. Each of these people had committed terrible acts to rise in position. Each and every one of the people around this table had committed terrible acts in order to survive. Understanding the score, he felt emboldened and continued.

"I knew I had to move. The problem was, I couldn't remember where I was in the village. I was paralyzed with fear for a minute. I knew one wrong turn here would have me beheaded on social media. I started hearing movement outside the hut, and one of the insurgents was yelling orders in Arabic only a few yards away. I grabbed the kid's *araqchin* with the white turban wrapped around it still. The fit was snug as hell, but it would do the trick. I wanted to strip out of my uniform and squeeze into the kid's *abaya,* but should a rescue mission be set in motion, I didn't want to look like just another enemy combatant. I needed to be identified by my men and wearing traditional Islamic clothing was probably not a great way to go about it."

"So, you get out of the hut?" Ronda asked.

"Yeah, I slipped out without incident but made a wrong turn and ended up walking right into the village bazaar. Normally, when violence broke out, most of the civilians in the town took cover. For some reason, every God damn villager was standing in the open-air market, and I was standing out like an ink spot in a bowl of milk. I froze when the yelling started and was able to get behind a wall for cover immediately following the first bullet that whizzed past my ear. I knew I was about to be completely surrounded and was working up the courage to stand up and take the easy way out in a hail of gunfire. As I stood and began to expose myself to death by firing squad, I could hear the familiar sounds of the M4 rifle. As you all know, the bad guys use Russian assault rifles. The two sounds of the weapons firing are incredibly different, so this was like music to my ears. I was facing the same direction as my attackers and saw the LATV speeding in with Paul on the .50 cal. The men were firing indiscriminately, laying waste to everything and everyone in the bazaar."

General Andrews interrupted Craig with a grunted chuckle. He folded his arms across his chest and leaned back in his chair. Craig knew that General Andrews knew exactly where this was going and found hearing the story firsthand a bit too much to bear. It wasn't every day General Andrews heard about the betrayal of the men who saved your life. That was a written rule and was unacceptable to someone like him.

"You didn't have to call me back in, General," Craig said, looking the man dead in his eyes.

"You were supposed to get the canister or get infected and die. You were never my choice for a real mission. You're an expendable asset that simply refuses to die."

Ronda and Katy both shot General Andrews looks that would stop an elephant in its tracks. Craig laughed at the general, mainly because he couldn't slap the shit out of him, and looked at Ronda for instruction. Ronda turned her stern gaze away from the general, softened her features, and asked Craig to continue.

"I made it into the LATV, and as we pulled out, I saw dozens of people sprawled out in the tiny marketplace. It looked like a few were injured, but the majority were not moving at all. Once we had made it out of the village and back to Bagram, we found a collection of MPs along with five or six agency men. My team was arrested, and I was shipped to Ramstein Air Base in Germany to undergo surgery on my hip."

"So what happened at the trial?"

"I was approached by a couple of three stars while still in Germany. They advised me that my rescue mission resulted in the deaths of over thirty-seven civilians. Furthermore, there were no enemy combatants found or even any evidence that a two-way firefight occurred. I started to question their report but was quickly put in my place. They told me they knew about the kid I had stabbed and that they knew a way everyone would get out of this 'minor' incident. I bought it, like a fucking moron, and did what I was told. I showed up to the trial, gave my report to the tribunal, and was dismissed, meaning I was unable to attend any more of the trial. I was ordered to continue physical therapy and go about my life until a verdict was reached."

"How long did it take them to issue their verdict?" Katy asked.

"One day. I wasn't told anything for another two weeks, but apparently, they had made up their minds before the trial even. It was the two-week mark when I was approached again by the same three-star generals I had met in Ramstein. They told me, matter-of-factly, that the trial was over. The men were sentenced to life in prison, convicted of atrocities against a civilian population, and it was over. I turned in my retirement notice, knowing I had more than enough time to walk with my pension. It was a week later that I was called into an office with a colonel and two one-star generals. The snot-nosed colonel, I outranked by the way, informed me that I was a disgrace to the uniform and was immediately being dishonorably discharged, forfeiting my pension."

"I think that about catches us up," Ronda said.

The general softened his position a bit. He had the clearance to look into the incident, but he never had. Hearing Craig retell the story, General Andrews softened his posture a bit. He was starting to understand that Craig had been railroaded. Maybe he had him all wrong.

"Now tell me about your team," Ronda ordered.

# TWENTY FOUR

## MILITARY ONLY

**"I'M NOT ENTIRELY SURE WHERE** to start, ma'am," Craig said honestly.

Ronda glanced hurriedly around the room, indicating she was sarcastically hoping he was speaking to someone else.

"I mean, you have their dossiers. What can I tell you about them?"

"I also have the dossier on your last mission in Afghanistan. Was that the whole story?"

Craig constantly felt like a child in this woman's presence, but she was able to convey her strength, power, or authority without being disrespectful. Sarcastic but not a smart ass. He had come up against all types of people in his time. This short, petite woman wearing an all-black designer pantsuit was probably the most impressive he had ever seen. Good, bad, or ugly, Agent Alexander was moving up the list of people he respected. Most of the agency and military personnel he had known were happy to read the paperwork, assess the situation based on that limited and usually slanted information, and then take action. Since these "big thinkers" were not the ones getting shot at or blown up, not knowing the full story was not that big of a deal. So far, Ronda seemed to be truly unique in the circles they both ran in.

"Well, my guys were the best. We were the type that no matter the task, we would achieve the objective. Put obstacles in our way and watch those obstacles get obliterated. Every single man was great individually, but together we were unbeatable."

"That's the shit I can read in the dossier. Actually, that's the shit I *did* read in the papers. Tell me who these men are. What makes them tick?"

"Ah, you mean, how can you manipulate them?"

"No, she means when you dinosaurs are out in the wild are you going to flake out or can they handle the extreme circumstances of this unprecedented situation," Katy said.

Craig was also beginning to like Katy quite a bit. She was light and airy, wit came easy to her, and she was quick to yield it like a weapon. That was the surface Katy, though, Craig knew. He could see the look in her eyes, behind all the other bullshit distractions. General Andrews had the same look. Agent Alexander, every member of his team, and Craig all had the same look in their eyes. It made him laugh to himself because this was the first time he had put it all together. The fate of the world was, more often than not, in the hands of psychopaths that the rest of the world hopes they'll make the right decision. *How the fuck have we made it this far?* Craig wondered to himself.

"Fine. Let's start with Centwally Diaz, or Twiz, to us. Centwally was my second-in-command, but I kept him as our sniper when we needed one. His shooting ability was only matched by his intelligence. He was educated in private schools in New York City but had grown up poor as hell in Puerto Rico. Abject poverty is an education in itself, a different level of street smarts are required. Mix that education with an upper-class American education and you get a Centwally."

"A regular rags to riches story," Katy said with a sarcastic smile.

"I suppose so," Craig said, having no idea what that was. If the store was not in the mall he patrolled, he didn't know what it was.

Ronda shot Katy a warm glance, humored by Craig's ignorance more than her comment but urged Craig to continue.

"Centwally Diaz is everything you could want in combat. If I go down out there, he is the one I trust to guide the team the rest of the way through. His patience is his greatest virtue though. This is what also makes him such an amazing sniper. He once waited over a week in the desert because we had a tip on Bin Laden.

Nothing happened, but we had to drag Centwally out. He was a hundred percent dedicated to his team and the mission."

"If pushed, would he choose his team or the mission?" Ronda asked.

"That depends on the mission, ma'am."

"Fair enough," Ronda replied. "Tell me about Armando Russo?"

"We called him Mondo. He was probably my best friend on the team. He was our corpsman, really a great medic. The irony was he never wanted anything to do with medicine. He grew up in a tough neighborhood in upstate New York and wanted to be the toughest guy around. He was the smartest guy on the block, however, and studied medical journals in order to learn about pressure points, why shredding a muscle was better than breaking a bone, and why it was more painful for someone to break their second knuckles instead of their first?"

"Why is it more painful?" Katy asked quizzically.

"Hell if I know. I was always too afraid to ask out of fear he would show me," Craig laughed.

"His parents were the classic Italian immigrants that came here, worked hard, and raised a family the 'American' way. He carried that sense of loyalty with him, which made him everyone's best friend on the team. He was the guy that would lay down to form a bridge for everyone else to walk over."

"Why wasn't Russo your second-in-command in that case?" Ronda asked.

"Respect and fear go hand in hand in two professions. The military and the mafia. Armando had everyone's respect, but since he was so close to everyone, nobody feared him. I was worried that when the shit hit the fan, his orders may be questioned. That is unacceptable."

Ronda slapped Armando's file on top of Centwally's on her left-hand side. On her right, she picked up a fresh file. "Let's talk about Timothy Willard."

"Big Tim was the team's wildcard. He is also a bit of a giant, standing six foot five inches. He grew up in a small town in Ohio. We instantly bonded over our love for central Ohio college athletics, both of us being Midwestern boys and all. He looked like a fucking model and was ragged on incessantly about it. Tim, however, had a dark side. He was written up twice for marijuana and would have been dishonorably discharged except for the team. He handled our demolition. When it came to most things, Tim was largely uneducated, but the guy had a brain for chemistry, unlike anything I'd ever seen. The guy would take damn near anything combustible and figure out a way to take down a building. Big Tim was great in combat, but the downtime was his cross to bear. He could not stay out of trouble. In the shit, though, he could not be outfought and was as tenacious as they came."

"He sounds like the honey badger," Katy noted.

"The honey badger?" Craig asked, confused.

"Dude, everybody knows about the honey badger."

"I literally have no idea what you're talking about," Craig said, confused.

"Christ, Ike, even I know this one," Andrews said, dismayed.

"You've got to see this video! It's awesome," Katy said, digging in her pocket for her phone.

"Maybe we can do all that once we're done with the Queen of the Dead?" Ronda asked, rhetorically, of course, as she picked up the second to last file on her pile.

Craig, not needing to be prompted further, began his report.

"Lou Noble was the heart and soul of the team. He played football in college, but after 9/11, he dropped out and enlisted. His exceptional athleticism got him through boot camp with no issues, and he quickly made a name for himself after he saved the entire platoon by locating and taking out multiple RPG teams that had surrounded their camp. I'm not sure what's in your file, but the guys that were there, they say he broke off of the team and used his knife to take them all out. When he returned, he was covered in blood, mud, and guts. Not one bit of it was his. Not even a scratch. Lou was the guy who set a goal and achieved it at all costs. When we were not in combat, Lou was like a celebrity. His fifteen minutes of fame in college gave him stories for days and the guys who couldn't stand to watch whatever second-rate action movie we had on VHS for the eight hundredth time ate it up. He grew up in Chicago's infamous Cabrini-Green housing project. The pushers and hustlers in the area identified his talent early and refused to let him get caught up in any of their bullshit. This made him, later in life, do the same for some of the other enlisted guys that were from the same circumstances. He would never say it out loud, but I know Lou took great pride in mentoring the other men whether they were black, white, or whatever."

Ronda nodded, laid Lou's file on top of the others, and picked up the final file with her right hand. She shook her head a bit as she flipped through it and then asked Craig to start before picking her eyes up again.

"Paul DiBernardo was built to be a soldier. He grew up outside of Boston, a typical middle-class Irish/Italian family from New England. He is the perfect size and weight, speed, accuracy, mental acuity, etc. He is right down the middle, a soldier before anything else. Dibo's problem, as I saw it, was that he was an opinionated hothead. Paul was virtually incapable of keeping his opinions to himself, regardless of the situation. He is as big on respect and loyalty as anyone else on the team, if not more. He was a fantastic wheelman and could keep his head through the worst of the worst. My guess is that since being incarcerated, he has not taken well to prison life. A prison guard barking orders at you was very different from a lieutenant, a major, so on up the ranks giving you commands. Most of the team arguments involved Dibo, but we all knew he was the first to apologize and was always accountable and reliable. He was the only guy on the team that got married in between our tours. I let him stay on the team because we are better with him than without him and because he's our brother. You can't replace that."

"Well, you definitely know your men. Paul has been involved in four incidents with the guards. In the first two, he hospitalized three guards, and he must be slowing down because, in the third fight, he only sent one guard to the medic. And the last one only had a black eye and bloody lip," Ronda said, confirming Craig's assumptions.

"He's not slowing down. He just got bored," Craig retorted.

"Oh, I'll be sure to remember that," Ronda replied, offending Craig with her carefree tone.

"So, are we wrapped here? What's next?"

"You are, Craig. You haven't told me about yourself yet."

"Well—" Craig had begun but was interrupted by someone behind him.

"He's a disloyal, unthankful, backstabbing, mother fucking piece of trash," a loud voice said from behind him.

Craig turned to see Paul and the rest of the boys behind him.

Katy turned her attention back to Craig and said, "Oh, this is gonna be fun."

# SECRET MISSION TWENTY FIVE

**BYRON POTTS HAD BEEN FOLLOWING** Aaron around the two-acre compound since Aaron had taken him in three years ago. The people in town did not understand him like Aaron did. They called Byron stupid, dumb, and slow. He was, he knew, but it was just something you didn't say out loud. Aaron treated him like a man. Aaron gave him odd jobs to do around the compound but never degraded him. He even never had Byron clean the toilets.

"That's women's work, Bryon," Aaron would always say, a warm smile stretching wide across his face.

Last night, however, Aaron gave him the most important job of all. Aaron sent Byron into Helm's Hamlet as a spy. He was told to just watch everyone and everything that had been going on. There had been a "commotion" on the HAM radio that Aaron kept in the communications building. Byron wasn't allowed in there because Aaron told him it was far too complicated. Byron didn't mind. He didn't like the smell or taste of the meat anyway and could not understand why anyone would build a radio out of ham.

Byron did as he was told, like he always had, and sat on the rooftop of Nate's Ye Olde Hardware Store in the town center. There was a maintenance ladder in the back of the building nobody used and old man Heffler couldn't hear anyway... neither could Mrs. Heffler, for that matter. Byron packed his thermos with the leftover vegetable soup from three nights earlier, a canteen of water on his belt, and headed out for the two-mile walk. His secret mission was made easier by the fact that there seemed to be no power in town. What Byron saw was as terrifying as it was confusing.

"All them peoples we roundeded up and made go in the church last night. Remember? For the sleepover?" Byron asked.

Aaron ignored the question and pressed Byron for more information. Byron relayed that a bunch of scary monsters had surrounded the church and then stormed the holy building in unison. Byron described the screams as best he could. What he lacked in verbal skills was relayed by the scars of the night wore on his face. As he kept covering his ears and rocking while trying to accurately report the horrors he had witnessed, he tried incredibly hard not to cry. He knew the other guys would make fun of him if he cried.

"Did anyone come out of the church?" Aaron asked, leaning closer to Byron and placing a hand on his knee to calm him down.

Byron sniffed and said, "Them monsters cames out. They looked like them people, and I almost shouted to them because I was so scared, but I member'd you said I was a spy."

"You're my number one spy. Don't you forget again, now. You did good, Byron. Keep going," Aaron said in a calm and nurturing manner.

Byron continued his story about the monsters. When they left the church, the monsters just stood there, and then Byron said he heard a loud shriek from somewhere in the distance. The monsters then began to walk down Main Street and started to spread out like they were looking for something.

"How long did you stay up on that roof?" Aaron asked, this time more matter-of-fact and business-like.

Byron tried to mimic his friend, sat up straight, and said, "I was scared. I stayed untils I heard the car."

"What car?" Aaron asked.

"It was the good guys, the soldiers. They had an army truck and wents into the church. I tried to warn them but I'ms a spy. I said nothing."

He went on to describe the monsters coming back, the soldiers leaving a man behind, one of them being eaten, and the other breaking into the hardware store. Byron said that he got nervous sitting on the roof and that he thought the soldier may be there to arrest him, so he climbed down and walked toward the big fire. The most notable thing Byron had said was how the abandoned soldier killed one of the monsters.

"What did you see at the fire?" Aaron asked.

He already knew of the fire Byron described and the airplane that had crashed earlier in the day. He just wanted Byron to feel special and useful. The compound was close enough that they could hear the loud explosions and felt a tremor when the aircraft lost its battle with gravity.

"I seent the soldiers dead in the army truck. No more monsters, though," he replied, a sigh of relief following his last statement.

"And then you came home at sunrise? Nothing else?"

"I seent that soldier again. The one that killed the monster. He drove the army truck away. I thoughts he heard me, but I hide better than anyone."

Aaron stood up, careful not to let the other men see the tiny smile forming at the corners of his lips. As he turned to face them, he made sure his face showed outrage.

"You see, brothers. The government sent these things to wipe us out. The military has abandoned us, and now an untold number of good, God-fearing, white United States citizens are dead. This is why we are here. This is why we train. We will free this town and show the world that God's Proud Americans are not some militia. We will show them that our way is the only way. WHITE POWER!" Aaron shouted, raising his right fist into the air.

# TWENTY SIX
## SPECIAL OPS

**CRAIG WAS NEVER ONE TO** take a punch. He knew plenty of guys that had, especially when owed to them, would allow the freebie punch to take place. More often than not, the situation was over. Unable to see the tactical advantage of that strategy, Craig had begun to set himself in a defensive posture had Paul began to swiftly move toward him. Craig had calculated three large strides until Paul would be on him. The second stride from his attacker made Craig rise from his chair and bend his knees, keeping his base strong. As Paul was making his third and final step, Katy leaped from her chair, grabbed Paul's left arm with both of her hands, and used his own momentum to flip him over onto his back.

"Who the fuck is that? Your daughter?" Paul asked Craig, gasping for breath.

"Hi, I'm Katy," she said with a smile.

"Would you all take your seats, please?" Ronda asked, extending her arm out and showing the empty chairs gathered around the table.

The rest of the boys moved suspiciously while Tim and Lou helped Paul back to his feet. Everyone, including Paul, sat down a few moments later. Ronda introduced herself, Katy, and just for laughs, General Andrews and Craig.

"Why are we here, lady?" Paul asked.

"Well, Paul, we have an apocalypse-level emergency that requires a team with your skillset and ability to get the job done quickly and quietly."

"First, my name is Paul. Second, you're a few years too late for that team shit. In case you didn't get the memo, that fuck right there retired us." Paul said, pointing at Craig.

"Jesus Christ, Paul, shut the fuck up and let the lady speak," Centwally said, not bothering to look at his friend.

"Thank you, Mr. Diaz. Now, here is the deal. If you survive your mission, you are free men."

"Free?" Armando asked, "No questions asked?"

"Well, you'll be out of prison. We'll have to see about the no questions asked."

"If you all find that agreeable, I will continue."

Nobody said anything, so Ronda continued with her briefing. She explained the drilling in Russia, the United States, and China, The Plagues, and the subsequent plane crash. With everyone still silent, Ronda explained that Craig would continue the briefing.

"Why is *he* here?" Paul asked before Craig could open his mouth.

"He's here because *he's* the only person on this planet to face one of these biological nightmares. Not only did *he* survive, but *he* also managed to kill one in the field. His knowledge is more valuable right now than any of us in this room, especially if you want to survive."

"Well, go ahead, hotshot. Tell us how you're going to keep us all alive. Let me guess, you got our backs," Paul shot at Craig with fire in his eyes.

Craig stood up and tried to speak but found his voice trapped somewhere in his throat. It had been so long since these men had been assembled in this fashion. He was looking at the faces of all these people that had once depended on him. Their freedom was dependent on him again. Craig looked down at the table and put his hands on the edge to steady himself. He closed his eyes, took a deep breath, and began his report.

When he had finished, the stone-cold looks he had received when he had first started speaking were now held in awe, mouths open wide in disbelief.

"So... vampires," Armando said, reluctantly

"No," Ronda stated emphatically.

"They sound like fucking vampires to me," Lou said, nodding his head toward Armando.

"First, vampires are completely fictional... as far as we know. Eve is a biological mistake. From what we have been able to tell, everything we found was never meant to be dug up."

"You named the thing in the coffin?" Paul asked, astounded.

"Why Eve?" Tim asked before letting Ronda speak.

"Because she's the first woman," Ronda replied.

Armando, being the team medic, asked, "So you're saying these things you found are like toxic waste and the people of Helm's Hamlet are the byproduct? Like a seagull covered in oil after an oil spill?"

"That is probably the most accurate simile I've heard to describe The Plagues."

"Wait a second," Tim started, "if this shit was dumped here and dumped forty-thousand feet below sea level? Who dumped it?"

"Since when do military men ask so many questions?" Katy asked

"We're not military anymore, young lady," Lou answered, showing the betrayal he felt for the first time.

"Listen! Do you understand? I mean, actually, comprehend what I'm telling you here today? None, not one of the three Plagues, could have possibly been put in the places they were found. This not only predates humankind. It predates the dinosaurs. Are you getting it? Something, close to a billion years ago, put three biological weapons into a container and dumped them on a largely lifeless planet," Ronda said.

Her normal calm and in-control demeanor was starting to show some wear and tear. She was hardly the first person to feel this way when attempting to brief Craig and his men.

"Okay, I'll bite. Where do you propose they came from?" Armando asked.

Ronda did not say a word. She simply looked up. Lou and Paul laughed. Armado, Centwally, and Tim all looked concerned. Craig was annoyed. Where they had come from was irrelevant. They were here, and now one of them was spreading some sort of virus to humans. Craig just wanted a gun and to be pointed in the right direction. It was then that he was betrayed by his own curiosity.

"So you're telling me that aliens used a prehistoric Earth as a toxic waste dumping ground but only left three? Why didn't they come back?"

"I said we have only found three. I never said there were *only* three."

# TWENTY SEVEN

**THE PRISONERS WERE ALL LINED** up, single file. The line of women were shivering, despite the warm afternoon in Helm's Hamlet. Men, some in leather vests with patches signifying their motorcycle club, others in military fatigues, were walking up and down the line with their rifles at the ready. None of the women looked up as they kept their arms folded across their chests.

"This city is under martial law. All of you have survived a horrible ordeal, and after tonight, you will no longer need to live in fear, thanks to God's Proud Americans. You will no longer fear illegal aliens crossing your borders. You will no longer fear that your government will leave you behind. You will no longer fear the creatures of the night. We are your saviors, and you will help rebuild a bigger and better Earth," Aaron proclaimed.

"March," a man at the front of the women barked as he put his left foot forward.

The ladies were marched in their single-file line, half a block until they were outside of the Iowa Credit Union. One of the men who had been marching alongside the women stepped forward and unlocked the front doors. Normally an alarm would alert the police to a possible break-in, but with the power in town out, no alarm was heard. In fact, with the police mostly dead, it wouldn't have mattered if the alarm worked or not.

"Why are you doing this?" a woman's voice asked, coming from the back.

"Brother Aaron told you. I ain't gonna repeat it," the man who led the march said angrily as he searched the line for whoever dared to speak.

"Bertrum Markus, don't you get loud with me. I know you. I know all of you! There's Ned Bowers and Travis French. What? Did you not think we'd recognize you, John David? You're the damn bank manager, and you took us to the bank. Now what is going on?" a middle-aged woman with long, curly brown protested.

Bertrum answered her queries with the butt of his rifle to her stomach. She crumbled to one knee and threw up what little food was in her stomach.

"I know you too, Bonnie Johnson. This isn't a Friday night at the bar no more. You don't sass me, you don't back talk me, you don't ask questions, and you don't say no. Got it?"

Bonnie was helped to her feet by some of the other ladies in line and did not say another word as they were escorted to the back of the bank. She swore to herself that no matter how this life ended, she would kill Bertrum Markus, no matter what.

Bonnie was no stranger to the pains a man could cause a woman. In her youth, she had been a flirty bartender. Hopes and dreams were still an achievable reality for her... until she met her first husband. He oozed charm, and although he was twelve years her senior, he had the sex appeal of a pop star. Then, after the pomp and circumstance a wedding offers, he changed. Bonnie could do nothing correct and was constantly reminded of that with a belt, shoes, fists, or anything else that the son of a bitch could use to hurt her. It took seven long years before she was able to work up the courage. Now, she was alive while he had been declared legally dead. Of course, people would talk, but nobody could prove anything, especially since his body had never been found.

Her fond memories of vengeance were erased in an instant when she was snapped back to reality by the sound of the opening bank vault. The smell of piss and shit invaded the group's nostrils and a chorus of gagging and coughing followed. When she was able to focus, she saw what had caused the smell. Rather than stacks of money or important lockboxes, this bank's new currency was the surviving women of Helm's Hamlet.

"Jesus Christ, Travis. Why haven't you been giving 'em bathroom breaks?" Bertrum said, covering his nose and turning away.

"Aaron didn't say anything to me about bathroom breaks. You saying I should have assumed? You know what he does to those that try to know what he wants."

Bertrum rolled his eyes. He knew they were leading a revolution. He believed wholeheartedly in the cause, but the stupidity and cowardice of some of these men was almost too much to bear.

"Get that moron Byron to come and clean this up and start taking them to the bathroom every two hours," Bertrum ordered.

Travis started to ask, "Did Aaron—" before he was cut off by Bertrum.

"I'm ordering you. I'll inform Aaron and take responsibility. Go get it done. The rest of you, get these heifers in the stockades."

The women were pushed forward, none trying to resist until they were all in the vault with the other fifteen women. Some of the ladies began to cry, but the sound was cut off from the world when the heavy metal door closed.

# TWENTY
# EIGHT

**RONDA HELD HER ARMS UP** trying to calm the clamor around the table, and said, "Gentlemen, when you return, I will be more than happy to spend weeks going over the minutiae. Right now, however, it is 12:45 p.m. local time. Sunset is at 7:15 p.m. local time. One thing our intel and Craig's report confirm is these creatures are nocturnal. If Eve and her brood didn't just eat everyone else, her original twenty-four soldiers could very well have grown exponentially."

"Wait, did you just call the creatures 'soldiers'?" Craig asked, looking for clarification on her terminology.

"Yes, their behavior and hierarchy are not unlike ants. Like soldier ants around the queen, to be specific. We believe that's why they move in tandem the way they do. Their only purpose seems to be to protect and to serve Eve."

"So, they're the cops and Eve's Karen?" Paul asked sarcastically.

Everyone around the table, including Ronda and Andrews, laughed heartily for a few minutes. The seriousness of this briefing had put a thick malaise over the room. Paul's ability to cut through that like a knife was appreciated by all.

"So, are we hunting these drones in their hive, or are we setting them up for an ambush when the sun sets?" Lou asked, starting to take some notes with the pad of paper and pen in front of him.

"We're not doing either of those things. This is a rescue mission," Craig answered.

"Hold up. A rescue mission? Who could be left to rescue?" Tim asked earnestly.

"The population of Helm's Hamlet is 637 men, women, and children. When our aircraft went down, we had reports that the tornado sirens began to go off throughout town. We have to assume the majority of the town went into their basements or cellars. Hopefully, they stayed put," Katy said.

"So you expect us to go house to house, knocking on cellar doors?" Tim asked, focusing his attention on Ronda.

"Yes. I expect you to clear that town of civilians so we can blow Helm's Hamlet and those things off the face of the planet," Ronda replied.

She paused a brief moment, taking the time to look each man in the eyes. Confident they both understood and were on board, she moved on.

"Now that we're all caught up, I'd like to introduce you to your dates for this evening."

Katy got up from the table and returned with a cart full of briefcases a minute later. Craig noted that if those cases had guns in them, this five-foot two-inch woman was a hell of a lot stronger than she looked. Craig saw he wasn't the only one that thought that when she lifted the first case from the cart with ease and placed it on the table. Katy unlatched the locks and opened the case then noticed Paul and Centwally, the team's resident gun nuts, give each other a look of shock.

"This is a modified German assault rifle. We had to lower the magazine capacity and caliber in order to accommodate the ammunition. Based on Craig's intel, we've also added high-wattage UV lights right here. If they can be hurt by light, this will definitely do the job," Katy said as she lifted it from the case.

This was a German assault rifle, or GAR, used by infantry forces in numerous countries. The plastic-made firearm was lightweight, had an excellent fire rate of five hundred rounds per minute, and was known for its power and maneuverability. The question Craig had, however, was what ammunition would be necessary for them to modify a damn near perfect firearm.

On cue, Katy looked at Craig and said, "Incendiary rounds. The flammable rounds are too volatile to be packed into a .556 caliber weapon at thirty rounds per magazine."

"Since when did incendiary rounds adhere to the Geneva Convention?" Armando, ever the medic, asked.

Ronda replied this time, saying, "I'm not here to answer stupid questions. The point is, you all get one of these little darlings as your dance partners tonight. We also have sidearms retrofitted for you all to carry the same rounds and caliber."

"What caliber round are we talking about here?" Lou asked.

"They take .22 long rifle bullets," Ronda answered, a bit sheepishly.

"C'mon!" Paul said, his frustration bubbling over.

"These bullets can literally set your target on fire, and you bunch of pussies are mad about the size of the round? Are you all trying to compensate for something?" Katy asked, holding her pinky finger up and wiggling back and forth.

"She's right," Craig said. "These will get the job done and scare the other drones away. Even if we run into Eve, we can put her down too and end this whole fucking thing."

"I got one last surprise for our sniper, over here," Katy said, motioning at Centwally.

She lifted a larger case onto the table with the same ease as she had the original. She opened it to expose a .50 caliber sniper rifle. Centwally's eyes grew to about the size of softballs.

"This rifle has not been modified. You get the full power of a .50 caliber round. That said, we did modify some bullets, though."

"Incendiary?" Centwally asked excitedly.

"No, the power of the rifle would cause the round to explode before it left the barrel, unfortunately. You'd basically catch on fire before your target would. The technology necessary to make that happen doesn't exist yet."

"Well, nobody's perfect, I suppose," he replied with a wink.

A collective groan was let around the table. Centwally was the team's "ladies' man," if such a term still exists. He actually couldn't help himself. He was just a flirt, not in the creepy pervert way but more in the way your best friend flirts with your girlfriend. There is nothing behind it, just a different type of camaraderie, at least in his mind.

Katy ignored him and continued, "We added extra, incredibly thin but strong casings around the bullet. This means your round won't be damaged upon impact. One bullet could literally rip through the skulls of seven men and still have a pristine bullet left. Hell, if you needed to, you could shoot through any metal on this planet."

Centwally nodded in approval. Katy looked up at Ronda to indicate she was done with her weapons presentation. The rest of the men followed her eyes back to Ronda and waited.

"So, we ready to suit up?" she asked.

Everyone but Paul stood up. Centwally bumped him in the shoulder with his elbow after a second, but Paul didn't move. Time stood still for a minute or two before Paul finally stood up.

"So, this is what we do now? We kill monsters?"

Lou said, "It beats twenty-three hours a day inside an eight-by-eight jail cell."

Paul looked at Craig and said, "I'm not doing this. I was a soldier, and now I'm prisoner 6032769601. Do you think the promise of freedom is enough to make me trust you? I would've died for you, and you almost did. I got life in prison for doing so. Now you want me to fight monsters with you... with experimental weapons? Send me back to jail for the rest of my life. I'm out."

The team all started to try talking some sense into Paul, but he insisted his mind was made up. Ronda did not wait for him to say no again and called for the MP.

Once he arrived, Ronda said, "Shackle the prisoner and escort him back to his transport. Contact the warden to let him know he's got one returning. Make sure he has transportation standing by for the prisoner. I'm not paying for another helicopter ride."

The young MP stood behind Paul and asked him to follow him back to the airplane. Paul wished everyone luck, except for Craig. He told Craig to fuck off and wished him a painful death.

Craig looked at Ronda and asked, "Was all of that necessary?"

Ronda shrugged her shoulders before turning her attention back to the full table.

"If nobody else is leaving, it's time to suit up. It's past time we clocked in. We're burning daylight."

# SECRETS INSIDE

# TWENTY

# NINE

**AARON COVE SAT IN THE** mayor's office, a sense of pride swelling up in him as he lit his cigar and put his feet on the mahogany desk. He had been predicting this day would come since he had left the National Guard five years ago. If he were being honest, when he said he left the service, he meant he was dishonorably discharged. Unceremoniously dropped because he had told his truth, but today, he felt like a prophet. His men had completely taken over the town of Helm's Hamlet and had almost every woman and girl left in town locked away in the bank's vault... just for now. His plans did not stop at taking control of the town.

"Brother Aaron, we have achieved our goal. All them bitches have been rounded up and are locked away," Bertrum said, interrupting Aaron and inflating his own ego.

"Good job, Bert. Anything else?"

"Can I ask you a question, sir?"

"Please do, soldier," Aaron replied.

"What is the long-term plan? What are we gonna do when the government sends their goons here?"

Aaron chuckled a little bit and sat upright in the leather chair. He wanted to show Bert just how put upon he was because of this question. Questions made his men less effective. What Aaron said had to be the same as God. You simply do not question God. Aaron closed his eyes and deeply sighed before he spoke.

"The long-term plan is simple. If Byron is to be believed, the military bugged out. These creatures have eaten everyone they could. What men were not eaten, have been shot or have joined us. The women are safe and sound in the bank vault. When resources disappear, animals always move on to another location. Tonight, I'm betting that the creatures will clear out, probably hit Adams or Indian Falls first. Then it's not our problem at all."

Bertrum nodded and smiled. He admired his leader, not only for his gumption but his intelligence. Bertrum's military experience had ended after ROTC in high school. After his recruitment, at eighteen, he was deemed Section Eight by the head shrinkers. He never even had made the rank of private before he was shipped back home with the other "rejects." Aaron took him in, trained him to do more than just march, and now he was a trusted lieutenant in the first army to occupy a United States city since the War of 1812.

Aaron sighed again and asked, "How are the women behaving?"

Bertrum smiled and said, "They are falling in line. You were right, a good shot in their stomach and they wouldn't say shit if they had a mouth full of it."

"You didn't hit them in the face, did you?"

"No, sir! You said no visible marks, and my men followed your orders to the letter."

Aaron thanked his trusted lieutenant and dismissed him, allowing Bertrum to return to his assigned duties. Before he could turn toward the door to leave, Aaron asked Bert to stick around for one last second.

"Better safe than sorry," Aaron said with a wink.

Bertrum was confused until he saw the walkie-talkie in Aaron's hand.

"Eagle Two, status report?"

The walkie was quiet for a second. The silence in the room was growing awkward when the static from the other end made Bert jump.

"Eagle One, this is Eagle Two. Over."

Aaron rolled his eyes and repeated himself, "Status report?"

"Eagle One, we have an armored vehicle heading toward town. Departure was one minute and twenty-two seconds ago. ETA, fifteen minutes."

"Roger that. Come on back home now, Eagle Two. Eagle One, over and out."

Aaron looked up at Bertrum and said, "You were right. Looks like Uncle Sam hasn't given up on our small town just yet. How about you gather a few men and meet this vehicle before they get into the town center. Advise them we have the situation under control. Let them know they have two choices: they may return home after they abandon their weapons and vehicle or join us."

"What if they fire on us?"

Aaron stared at his subordinate sternly. He knew he didn't have to say another word. Bertrum took the hint and turned to hurriedly leave the office before he was accused of insubordination. Aaron was not one to have his orders questioned, and those that did would face the harshest of consequences.

Aaron switched the channel on his walkie-talkie and began to speak, "Attention! We have incoming. All men take up defensive positions throughout town. Alpha unit, move to the bank and wait for further instructions."

**TIM BROUGHT THE HEAVY DUTY** Tactical Truck, or HDTT, to a full stop a quarter mile from the town line. The men climbed out of the massive 8x8 transport vehicle, moved around to the back, opened a hatch, and pulled their rifles from inside. They also made sure to grab the ammo boxes containing extra magazines and all of the extra rounds they could hold.

Craig looked over everyone once they had assembled. He didn't realize just how much he had missed this. How much he had missed his men. The guilt he felt kept him from remembering anything but the bad times, but he'd be damned if he said he didn't miss this family.

"Alright, lock and load here. I want to hit that fucking town ready to fight. Centwally, I want you and Katy on that water tower," Craig said, pointing to the one hundred sixty-four-foot structure.

Katy began to protest, but Craig simply held a hand up, silencing her immediately. He took a deep breath and exhaled for a long exhale before continuing.

"My word is absolute. I don't want one fucking question from here on out. Execute my orders, or we will fail this mission. That's not happening again. Heard?"

The silent nods told Craig he could continue.

"Good. Now, Katy and Centwally, I want you two on that water tower. I want you constantly talking to us. Let us know everything you see, even if it's nothing. Tim, you stay in the driver's seat.

Mondo and Big Lou, you are on foot, flanking us and searching the homes on the fringe of town. I want you to stick together and rendezvous with Tim and me in the middle. We will clear the business and apartments in town."

"Roger that," the team replied.

"Remember, we are searching for survivors here, but our mantra still stands: If anyone or anything becomes a problem, remove them from the equation. Do not fire unless fired upon. Comms will stay open, so don't be stingy with the intel. Stay frosty, work together, and we can do this. Heard?"

"Hooah, mother fuckers!" Lou chanted to the team.

Craig could see the change in the team. Someone had just flipped their switch. He was no longer looking at fractured men. These guys were back. Back to being soldiers. Back to being professional badasses. Back to being exactly what they were meant to be. Katy was still smiling that bright smile, which was scarier than the looks in the eyes of the men.

"Let's move out!" Craig barked.

Centwally and Katy began a faster than normal jog through the cornfield on their right, making a beeline for their elevated position. Lou and Armando began walking to the left, through another field of corn, where they would wind their way around the edges of town before entering from the rear. Tim and Craig climbed back into the heavy, armored vehicle, with Tim driving, and began to push slowly into Helm's Hamlet.

As the vehicle inched closer to town, Tim could start to see the making of a roadblock. He turned to Craig, who had also noticed the obstruction, and advised Tim to slowly approach.

"This can't be good," Craig muttered as they pulled up to the barricade.

"Can we help you, boys?" a bearded man asked, a rifle in hand.

Craig could see one other man in front of the roadblock was making his way to Craig's side of the vehicle. As he glanced around, careful to only move his eyes, he could see a few of the corn stalks moving unnaturally. The armor on the vehicle would protect them from any incoming fire, so long as these yocals didn't have an RPG or other explosive devices. Regardless, Craig wanted to avoid a firefight here.

"We are reservists from Kansas. We were activated by your governor for a rescue mission," Craig lied.

Tim saw the bearded man's attention focus on Craig and took the opportunity to remove his sidearm and place it, at the ready, on his lap.

"Rescue mission? Do we look like we need to be rescued?"

"No, you men look like you could handle damn near anything. Unfortunately, we need to satisfy the brass. Let us just do a quick sweep through town. You know how it is..."

The bearded man appeared to be thinking for a second before he said, "Gentlemen, we're going to need you to step out of the vehicle, please."

"And then you'll take us through town?" Craig asked, playing dumb.

The bearded man shook his head and spit off to his left, "Naw, sir. How 'bout y'all just get out."

Craig acted like he was considering this when he finally heard Centwally's voice in his ear, "Ike, we are in position. I'm fire ready. Just give the word."

"You got it," Craig complied with a nod toward Tim. Without the hostiles knowing it, Craig was also communicating with Centwally and Katy.

Both men exited the HDTT, sure to leave their rifles in the can of the truck. Two men ran out of the cornfield and held rifles on Tim and Craig as the bearded man, who had done all of the talking, lowered his.

"My name is Lieutenant Bertrum Markus with God's Pure Americans. Do y'all know what happened here last night?"

"No? What?" Craig asked, confused, playing dumb as he looked at Tim.

"Well, long story short, the government sent in some sort of creature to take us out. We stopped them after the monsters ravaged our town and have finally taken back control of the town. I was ordered by our leader, Brother Aaron Cove, to make you boys an offer."

"Oh, yeah, what kind of offer?"

"You boys have two choices because Brother Aaron is a kind man. You can leave your equipment, weapons included, and turn back for home. Your other choice is to join God's Pure Americans at the rank of private. You both look like strong men, though. I think you could rank up quickly."

Craig knew there was no good way this could end. These militiamen had the drop on them. Any move they made would get them shot. They didn't look like too much, but someone had trained these guys enough to know to keep their distance. This at least reminded Craig not to underestimate this group. It also gave Craig another idea.

A year before the team had been first assembled, Tim and Craig had been working on a black ops mission in Columbia. The cartel knew that at least one of the men was working undercover for the American government. Had they both continued to protest their innocence, they both would have been tortured and killed. Craig and Tim knew one of them had to confess. In an epic rant, Craig expressed his love for God and country. He was about to have multiple impromptu amputations, performed with a rusty machete no less, when Tim shot him. The two rounds Tim had put into Craig's chest were perfectly placed, missing any major organs. Tim was tasked with getting rid of the body, which he did, but at a secret US military base located outside of Bogata. Due to this sacrifice, Tim was welcomed into the organization, and the pair burnt the entire operation down a month later. Craig only spent a week in recovery. That wasn't such a bad price to pay.

"Well, boys? What's it gonna be?" Bertrum asked, snapping Craig out of his flashback.

"It's a great offer, but this is the United States, not Columbia," Craig said, glancing at Tim.

Tim's face registered a moment of confusion before Craig saw he understood. In a flash, Tim pushed Craig to get his back to him, pulled Craig's sidearm from its holster, and fired three rounds into Craig's back. The men in the militia all jumped back and froze for a moment, a lucky break for Tim. Had they been better trained, they would have shot him before he had a chance to level his gun up to aim at Craig.

"Jesus Christ, boy! What in the fuck did you just do?" Bertrum asked, startled.

"He was never going to go with you. I've heard all about you guys. I'm a big fan. I'm a brother with a similar organization in Kansas. Let's do this!" Tim said excitedly.

Bertrum got into the passenger seat of the truck and told Tim to drive. He had instructed his other men at the roadblock to load the materials into their truck and follow them back into town. Tim did as he was instructed, and in a few seconds, he and Bertrum were en route to the mayor's office to meet Aaron.

Once all of the vehicles had pulled away, Craig shot up from playing dead. The pain in his back was intense. The twenty-two caliber rounds hitting his vest didn't amount to much, and he was sure he felt more pain stubbing his toe in the middle of the night. The burning metal, caused by the incendiary round, on the other hand, felt like he was being bitten by a colony of ants. Craig heard Centwally and Katy laughing in his earpiece. They were quick to let the rest of the team know that he was doing the potty dance while trying to remove his vest.

Vest off and shirt back on, Craig said into his communicator, "This town is red hot. Assume everyone is hostile. Tiny is embedded, be mindful of your targets. I'm proceeding into town on foot."

# CONCEALED

# THIRTY
# ONE

**ARMANDO AND LOU HAD MADE** their way around to the back of the town. They had checked a few farmhouses and their cellars but found nothing. It was their fourth check that left them both shaken up. The house had been burnt down, and the cellar door, about fifty feet away from where the main house had once stood, was wide open. As they approached, Lou identified a body lying just outside the door, one foot still inside the opening.

"Mondo, we got a body," Lou said.

Armando quickly came over to check but was warned by Lou that the man lying face down may not be a man anymore. With the remainder of these creatures in play, he took more caution in rolling the body over. Mondo was relieved the body was just a human, but his relief quickly faded.

"This man was shot. Two in the chest, both look like front entry wounds. He has one more wound on the back of his head. It looks like he was shot up close after he had fallen."

Although he could hear the report on his communicator, placed firmly in his ear, Craig didn't register too much concern. They knew a hostile force had taken control of the town. A dead guy was not that surprising. It wasn't until Armando and Lou reported the same scene seven more times after seven different homes had been searched. Every victim was a man, shot twice in the chest and once in the head.

"What the fuck is going on, Ike?" Centwally asked, his voice a bit shaky.

"I've got no idea."

"Ike, Tiny has reached the town center. They are parked outside of the town hall. I count twenty targets."

"Keep an eye on them, but Tim knows what he's doing."

Craig only now thought about how fortuitous it was that Tim had been the one in the truck with him. While each man was capable in their own right, Tim was the only one that had the clandestine experience to effectively infiltrate this group and gather the necessary intelligence they needed to complete the mission.

"Well, they aren't very good. I could take most of them out right now," Centwally noted.

Katy came over the comms for the first time, asking, "Mondo, say again. You found seven male bodies, correct?"

"Affirmative."

"Were they wearing wedding rings?" Katy questioned him.

"How the fuck would I know?"

"Katy, what's the point?" Craig asked.

"Seven farms, seven dead men. Where are all the women?"

Immediately, every member of the team had the worst possible images enter their minds. Having served in almost every war-torn country on Earth, everybody on the team knew that the women in the civilian population took the real brunt of war. Death was not the worst part of war. Craig's anger rose, and although he knew better than to act out of emotion, he could not help himself.

"I want eyes on any females. ASAP. All teams consider any man to be hostile."

# THIRTY

# TWO

## DO NOT SHARE

**TIM WAS ESCORTED INTO CITY** hall and taken up a flight of stairs. Before entering the set of doors marked with a painted sign that read: "Mayor Trask," he was relieved of his sidearm, knife, and frisked one last time. The guard found the .38 revolver tucked inside his ankle holster and took it from him as well. The guard held it up in front of Tim with a grin, letting Tim know he was unable to get anything past him. After a nod from the guard, Tim was permitted entry into the office.

A tall, skinny man was standing up behind the mayor's desk. The room stunk of cigar smoke and body odor. Tim had smelled far worse, though, and moved toward the desk. When he got within three feet of the mahogany workspace, he stopped. Tim adjusted his posture to stand at attention and saluted. Tim seemed to have hit the mark as the man on the other side of the desk smiled, mimicked Tim's posture, and returned the salute as a commanding officer did.

"At ease, soldier," Aaron said.

Tim relaxed his posture slightly and put his arms behind his back.

"What's your name, son?"

"Private Tim Willard," he replied honestly. Tim was certain this guy would not be alive long enough for it to make any difference.

"Brother Aaron, this man wishes to join the GPA," Bertrum said.

Aaron smiled again and asked Tim, "Is that so?"

Bertrum answered before Tim could, "He shot and killed the man with him. Said he was with a similar group out in Kansas."

"It's always nice to meet another dedicated brother of the cause," Tim said, puffing his chest with pride.

Aaron nodded his head for quite some time while he was thinking. He stopped only when he was ready to speak and smiled that same creepy smile at Tim while speaking to Bert.

"You two can take over guard duty at the bank. Bert, you'll show him the ropes. Make sure he gets his sidearm back. You can keep his rifle, and I'll keep the other one. I don't think his friend will be needing anymore. Relieve Ned and Travis. Tell John David, I need him here to go over some of these files."

Aaron then asked Tim, "That all sound good to you, son?"

"Yes, sir," Tim said, standing stiff again and saluting.

He waited until Aaron returned his salute before he turned and left the office with Bertrum leading the way. Bert gave Tim back his sidearm and revolver. He admired the GAR that now belonged to him and instructed Aaron's guard that was posted outside of the door that the other GAR that they had brought inside should be turned over to their boss immediately. Satisfied the sentry understood his orders, Bertrum told Tim that he would have to stop at the bank. Confused, Tim followed but did not say a word.

Bert introduced Tim to a few of the men that were patrolling the streets. Tim listened to their ignorant hate speech about black people, the LGBTQ community, and illegal immigrants, reluctantly agreeing when he could fit a word in during their incoherent rants. With each person that opened their mouth, Tim envisioned a bullet going through the front of their skull. He said a silent prayer that he would be the one to get to take them out of this world.

Just when Tim thought he couldn't take it anymore, the pair arrived at the bank. The men in the street had gone back to performing their duties, thankfully leaving Tim in peace for the time being. Bert gave Travis, Ned, and John David the orders Aaron had bestowed upon them. The men didn't hesitate and eagerly ran out of the building, hoping to please their commander. Alone with Bert, Tim took the chance to ask a question.

"What are we doing at the bank, Bertrum? Are we really guarding the money?"

Bert looked angrily at Tim and said, "My name is Sergeant Markus. Mind your business and do your job."

Tim, surprised by this sudden turn, started to apologize before he was interrupted.

"I'm just kidding, man. You wanna see what we're guarding? Follow me."

Bert turned and motioned with his head for Tim to follow him with a wide smile on his face. Tim hadn't noticed until now that Bert's two front teeth were missing, with the remaining ones stained yellow. The pair were standing in front of the large metal vault. An awkward silence filled the room as Tim looked at Bert confused. Bert just smiled and took a necklace off from around his neck. He handed the makeshift keychain to Tim and told him it was the key with the green head. Tim was nervous as to what he would find behind the massive door. The thought of the look on Craig's face if Tim returned with no tangible intelligence was enough to make him fight through his nerves. He turned the lock and spun the five-spoked handle hard to the left. A few loud sounds, indicating the locks were releasing, and the door creaked open only a sliver.

"Go 'head, boy," Bert urged him along.

Tim repositioned himself in front of the crack and opened the door. Instinctively he got into a defensive posture, assuming one or more of the creatures were going to rush him. Instead, Tim saw a group of approximately one hundred women. They were dirty and huddled together, shaking more from fear than the temperature inside the vault.

"What the fuck," Tim asked, unable to control his mouth at that point.

"What'd you mean, boy? These are bitches. You do like pussy, don't you, boy?"

Tim remembered he was playing a character and snapped at Bert, "What you sayin' about me? Don't you question another man about that shit. You think I give a fuck?"

Bert held up his hands and smiled, "Alright, alright. Settle down, boy. You seem a bit shocked."

"Why are we keeping them here?"

Bert raised a suspicious eyebrow at Tim but did not speak.

"I mean, why we got all this pussy locked up? Shouldn't we be fucking 'em?" Tim asked.

Bert laughed. Rubbing his beard, he said, "You and I agree on that part, brother. Aaron says we can't, though. He wants to save them."

"Save them for what?"

"We're gonna trade 'em. He's been talking to our brothers in other towns and states. Everyone is on alert that these creatures are out of food here. Aaron thinks they gonna move on and try to find new food. When they leave, we take over the town. Our people are gonna be all that's left. You're looking at our new slave labor."

A few of the women gasped, which made Bert laugh. He walked into the middle of the women and held his hands out like a car salesman with a deal that was just too good to be true.

"Pick one, brother," Bert said, spinning around to demonstrate just how much product he had in stock.

The second his back was turned, Tim drew his pistol intending to shoot Bert square in the spine. As he did, the bell on the front door of the bank sounded, alerting everyone that someone had just entered. The distraction was just enough of the chance Bert had needed. He got his rifle to the ready before Tim had his shot with the pistol lined up. Bert smiled at Tim and was about to say something when Tim saw one of the women behind Bert stand up. In a smooth motion, the curly-haired woman pulled the pistol from the holster attached to the back of Bert's belt. Tim flinched when the first shot sounded, thinking it was meant for him. It took as long as it took Bert to fall to the ground before Tim realized he had not been shot. The next six bullets that the curly-haired woman fired did not make him react at all.

"I told him I would kill him," she said to no one in particular.

"Shoot him, Bonnie!" a couple of the women started to shout, pointing at Tim.

Tim thought he was screwed when Bonnie pointed the gun at Tim and said, "Freeze!"

He turned to run, unable to pull the trigger on any of these women himself, and ran into another person. The knife the man had been holding, no doubt ready to stab Tim in the back, fell to the ground. Tim grabbed the man by the throat, put his left leg behind the man's right leg, and pushed with all of his might. The man fell down in a heap and started crying, holding his head.

"Don't hurt him," Bonnie said as she rushed through the crowd of women.

"To hell with that, lady," Tim said as he put his own pistol against the man's forehead.

"He don't know no better. He's slow," Bonnie said.

Tim took a breath and observed the situation rather than reacting to it. The man on the ground was sobbing and screaming "owie" as he held his head. Tim looked Bonnie in the eyes, saw she was sincere, and told her to tend to the man lying on the ground. He ran over to the bank window and looked outside to see if anyone had heard the commotion. The streets were covered with men on patrol, but nobody was paying any attention to the bank.

"Ike, come in," Tim said, still standing at the bank window watching everything.

Craig came back on the comms after five seconds of silence and listened to Tim's report. Craig advised that he was nearing the town center but had to take cover or start to eliminate targets. Lou advised the team that he and Armando were on the north side of town and were waiting to proceed forward. Centwally told the team he was clocking targets both on the rooftops and on ground level. He would be able to clear a path for one of the teams but not all of them based on their relative positions around the town. With everyone in place, they waited on Craig to make the call.

# THIRTY
# THREE

**THE PRIORITY OF THIS MISSION** was to rescue survivors. They had identified every known survivor in Helm's Hamlet. They were the priority. Craig told the team as a whole that Centwally needed to clear a path for Tim. He was closest to the truck, he was in the most danger, and he had all of the survivors—at least the only survivors that would be left when they were done. Armando, Lou, and Craig would fight their way into the town center and meet up with Tim at the truck. When the team was clear of town, Centwally and Katy would meet up with the truck a mile down the road at the designated location.

With the plan in place, Katy began to identify targets for Centwally. Her role was to pick the order in which the targets would be taken out by the sniper lying prone beside her. The purpose of this was to allow the sniper to concentrate on the shot while the spotter made sure the order allowed for the easiest kill with the most amount of speed.

Centwally was instructed to start with the guy in flannel on the rooftop of the diner. He would then shift fifteen degrees and take out the man in camouflage on the roof of city hall, followed by the two guys pacing on the rooftop of Nate's Ye Olde Hardware Store. Katy noted his third and fourth shots would be coming with a change in the wind so he should adjust his sight up three and left two. Centwally confirmed the adjustment and inhaled deeply. As he began to exhale slowly, Centwally depressed the trigger. The butt of the heavy rifle flung itself into his shoulder on the recoil, but he was used to that feeling after ten years in the service. As planned, he moved left to right, dispatching each target with a single round. Katy confirmed each man was down while the other combatants on the ground had no idea what had happened.

"High ground is neutral territory again, Tim. You guys are all clear."

"Good work, you two. When you see Tim step out of that bank, I want you to start taking out ground forces as you see fit. You don't have the green light until then. Mondo and Lou, I want you two to move your asses. Get to that truck. Tim, get your package ready to move. Once you're lined up and ready to make the run, give Centwally the word."

"Roger that," Mondo said, speaking for Lou as well. They began to jog faster so they could get themselves into position.

Tim, as ordered, got the women inside of the bank ready to move. Much to his chagrin, Bonnie had let Byron leave out the back door. He had promised not to tell anyone and that he would go hide from everyone for the rest of the night. Tim was not sold but didn't have time to chase down Byron. He asked Bonnie to take up the rear of their caravan, telling her that he trusted her to take care of everyone. Bonnie reluctantly agreed and joked, but not really, that they had better not leave her.

With everyone inside the bank ready to go, Tim told the team that he and his new friends were ready to move. He took one step outside and ran into the guy that had introduced himself as John David. He smiled at first, only seeing Tim. When he saw the ladies following closely behind him and not trapped in the vault, his smile shifted to anger. Tim didn't give him time to react in any other way as he put his pistol under John David's chin and pulled the trigger.

"Anytime, Centwally!" Tim shouted.

Tim's long stride was his greatest asset right now as he started to sprint toward the truck parked less than a block away. He could hear the zip of the rounds Centwally pass right by his head. Using his peripheral vision, he could see the men he had met just an hour earlier get splattered. He could hear the women behind him running and screaming and kept yelling words of encouragement like: *"move your ass"* and *"hurry the fuck up."*

Craig was sprinting, sidearm in hand, as he saw Tim with the longest line of people he'd ever seen running behind him. He wasn't exactly sure how they would all fit on the HDTT, but he did know nobody was getting left behind today. From only a few yards away, Craig could hear the distinct sound of the GAR and knew Armando and Lou were about as close as he was to their meeting point. Everyone on the street, Craig and his team, the members of God's Pure Americans, the women running, or even Aaron watching all of this from his window in the mayor's office, did not notice the dark skies west of the town. There was a massive thunderstorm approaching and approaching fast.

The entire team was reunited at the HDTT within seconds of one another. Armando and Tim were ordered by Craig to load the ladies into the back of the truck. He and Lou were to lay down cover fire. To Craig's surprise, they were loaded and ready to go within a few minutes. Most of the heavy firing was being done by Centwally from the water tower. Craig and Lou had been firing rounds when necessary, but it was more to keep enemy combatants suppressed and in cover as opposed to attempting to kill anyone.

Tim tapped Craig on the shoulder, and he stood, knowing that meant they were loaded and ready to go.

"I'm out!" Lou shouted.

Craig turned around to hand Lou a new magazine when he saw two men come from Lou's left flank and tackle him. Armando jumped off of the truck's bumper, coming to Lou's aid. No sooner than he did was he fighting three other men that seemed to come out of nowhere. Craig took his knife out of the sheath on his belt and moved toward the small riot unfolding when he felt something hard crash into his back. He turned to see a man with a two-by-four swinging at his head. He managed to take the brunt of the force on his left forearm but still fell onto his back.

"Start the truck!" Craig shouted at Tim.

Tim did as ordered. Their assailants seemed unsure if Tim was on their side or not since Bertrum had introduced them and mostly left him alone. Centwally, helpless from his vantage point on the water tower, advised the team that he had no shot. The sound of Tim's .38 revolver began to ring out. The man that had been attacking Craig with a piece of lumber fell to the ground lifeless. With Craig on his feet again, he picked his knife back up and began to help Armando and Lou with their problems.

Craig had made three deep stabs into two men's kidneys before Lou had been able to get the upper hand on his other two assailants. Armando screamed in pain just as Lou and Craig had removed three men that had gotten on top of him. One of the men had bitten the tip of his index finger off. The man laughed as Armando jumped to his feet and pulled his knife out. Rapidly and repeatedly, Armando stabbed the man in the stomach until his entrails were falling out, with a slight assist from gravity.

"Damn, I knew we'd be just a little rusty," Craig said humorously.

The team did not have time to laugh, however, as a sharp ringing sound came from somewhere behind them. Katy identified the target on the second floor of city hall, and Centwally fired without hesitation.

"Jesus, that was close," Lou said, laughing again.

Craig looked down at the pinching pain in his ribs. The skin around the area began to feel hot, and he instinctively put his right hand over his lower rib cage on his left-hand side, his knife falling to the ground. He raised his hand up and saw the palm of his hand was covered in blood.

"Okay, so we're *all* really rusty," Craig said, showing the red liquid to everyone else as he fell to his knees.

# THIRTY
# FOUR

**ARMANDO LEAPED INTO ACTION, DESPITE** the fact that he was missing part of a finger. He removed the backpack from his shoulders, unzipped it, and began to bark orders as he put on his rubber gloves. In a combat situation, your rank means everything unless you are wounded. A wounded soldier and their commanders answered to the medic at that point, whether it was the commander-in-chief or a fresh out of college officer. Armando was now in charge of this situation.

"Centwally, you got a shot?" Tim asked, his gun trained on the broken window on the second floor of city hall.

"Adjust seven and three, two hundred and fifty-five meters, Centwally. Second floor, third window. Fire, fire, fire!" Katy called, seeing the man's head emerge.

Centwally confirmed his target and pulled the trigger. He saw his quarry's head snap back but saw no blood splatter on the wall.

"Why are you always getting shot, Ike?" Armando asked, joking with his patient.

"Maybe they know him?" Tim said, looking down at Craig.

Mondo said, "Centwally, can you confirm the kill?"

"Negative, Doc."

"Tim and Lou, get your asses in there. Clear it and confirm or kill that son of a bitch," Mondo said, not looking up from his work.

"Are you going to pass out again, you pussy?" Armando asked, trying to keep Craig jovial and thinking.

"Fuck no. Like I'd ever live that down," Craig replied, wincing in pain.

"Good, you're a man now, son."

"Quit making me laugh, asshole."

"Ahh, it was just to distract you. I've added a heavy blood coagulant to your wound. That should stop you from bleeding out. When we get home, you'll need a real doctor to remove any blood clots that may form."

"I'm not leaving."

"Nobody said you were. Now count to three."

"One—" Craig started but had his voice cut off midway to two.

"Okay, I didn't have any staples handy, so I have to use some safety pins. Bite down. We're not done yet," Armando said as he applied the next safety pin.

Lou and Tim emerged from the city hall building, shaking their head that Craig's would-be murderer was nowhere to be found.

"What do you mean he's gone?" Centwally asked, embarrassed that he had missed his shot.

"We have a bigger problem, Ike. Looks like a thunderstorm is heading in. I give us ten to fifteen minutes," Katy said, a shaky tone in her voice.

"It's rain, kiddo. Are you going to melt out there?" Tim asked sarcastically, laughing.

"No, stupid. Didn't you listen during the briefing? I'm worried about the clouds blocking out the sunlight."

# THIRTY FIVE

**THE TEAM COULD SEE THE** storm rolling in from the west. The thick black clouds were moving fast toward them. While the rest of the team had yet to experience the horrors of Helm's Hamlet after dark, Craig was in no hurry to be stuck here again. The thunder was getting louder and more frequent. Craig checked his watch. They had three hours left until actual sunset. Based on the speed and size of the storm, their timetable was now adjusted to ten minutes.

As the team began to move toward the HDTT, they could hear the sound of boots marching toward them. On the other side of HDTT, the massive truck was obstructing the team's view, were twenty members of the militia, fully armed. For a minute, Craig thought the monsters were coming and breathed a small sigh of relief when he saw it was just regular men.

"Are we still waiting until fired upon?" Tim asked excitedly.

Craig had to make a judgment call, but Ronda's voice broke in over the comms for the first time.

"Rules of engagement have changed. Take these fuckers out!" Ronda commanded.

The team, Craig included, needed no further warning. The first shot to ring out came from 350 meters away, as Centwally and his sniper rifle began to fire into the armed crowd. Armando, Lou, Tim, and Craig all formed in a line, like they were playing Red Rover, and began to plow the road.

Both teams found themselves in a reload close to the same time, and the remaining militiamen decided to charge, the distance between them shrinking as they advanced during the initial firefight. The team, in unison, dropped their rifles, pulled their sidearms from the holster on their belt, and began to fire. The incendiary rounds fired by the handgun were not as effective, resulting in everyone's gun jammed. With the mob closing in on them, they discarded the weapons and prepared themselves for hand-to-hand combat.

The militia was only ten men after the team had dropped a few dozen, but they swarmed the men like a hive of angry bees. Lou, the only black man on the team, seemed to be the main target of the men. They tried to pile on him, but Lou was swinging his patented haymakers, connecting with every jaw he aimed at. Armando was taking two guys armed with knives before he got stabbed in the right side. He fell to the ground and would have been murdered if Centwally, now with a clear shot, fired one round. Both men were killed in the blink of an eye.

Tim was handling two more with relative ease. One man with a ponytail threw a wild punch at him. When he missed, Tim grabbed the man by his long hair and violently threw him backward onto the ground. The man's skull would have made a fantastic sound when it hit the asphalt on Main Street if it weren't for Tim's Viking-like battle cry into the sky. As if Homer were writing an epic, a long line of lightning flashed behind him at the same time. If anyone had time to pay attention, Tim would have looked like a Greek god at that moment.

Ike was having some issues with the remaining men. They had been able to identify the wounds on his ribs and continued to punch the spot every opportunity they got. Centwally told Craig he had no clean shot, so he was not going to be very much help. He was down on one knee when a thunderous right cross caught him in the temple. His vision blurred, and his right ear began to ring. Summoning all he had left in the tank, Craig shot up in a fit of pure rage. He grabbed the closest person to him by the head and, with a shout, twisted the man's neck like it was a bottle cap. Not one to admire his handy work, Craig immediately moved to the man who had been punching his bullet wound, causing the blood to pour like water from a spout. His attacker threw one more punch. Craig caught the man's fist in his hand and bent it upward. The man's wrist, loose at first, began to snap, and he fell to one knee. Craig towered above him and, with his right hand, delivered the hardest punch he could muster directly to the man's right temple. Travis French collapsed dead, the side of his face noticeably smashed in. The last man who had been attacking Craig turned to run away, but once he had a clear view, Centwally took him out with a single shot.

The first few minutes following the brawl was the time to be selfish. Each man checked themselves for wounds and caught their breath. Armando was administering his own medical aid with the help of Lou and Tim. Craig pulled himself to his feet and looked around at the carnage. They had killed seven men with their bare hands, Centwally taking out the other three from a distance. The excitement of the moment was beginning to pass, and everyone's adrenaline was falling back to a normal level.

"We still got a job to do, guys. These ladies still aren't out of harm's way."

The sunlight, once shining down on the combat like a spotlight, began to fade away. It happened slowly, but to the team, it was far too fast.

"We gotta go! Now!" Craig commanded.

The team was now facing a sad reality. The truck could take all of the women but squeezing the team in was going to be difficult.

"We run out," Craig said, not hesitating.

"You and I can't," Armando said. "If we try, we both may bleed out before we hit the first cornfield."

Craig wanted to think for a few minutes, but the thunder reminded him that they were out of time. If they didn't move now, none of them would make it out of Helm's Hamlet.

"Tim, you're driving. Lou, you get Armando loaded on that truck."

"What about you?"

"I'll sit on someone's lap. I don't care, frankly. We have got to go right now."

Lou almost had Armando on board when the hideous screeching and hissing, like the sound of a tea kettle, broke out, seemingly covering the town like a blanket. Every single person stopped what they were doing and listened for a second. Thirty seconds later, a chorus of replies sounded out in the form of screeching and hissing.

Craig shouted, "Tim, start this big bitch up! Let's roll!"

Everyone was on board, with Armando in the passenger side seat and Lou cramped into the truck bed. Craig jumped on the foot rail under the passenger side door and held onto the side mirror, his arms laced around the metal frame like a snake.

Craig shouted, "Go, go, go!"

Tim pushed down on the gas pedal, and after a little more force, the fully loaded armored vehicle began to set out for home. But shortly down the road, Tim spotted an obstruction a few hundred yards away.

"It's not an obstruction. It's them," Katy said, still on the water tower with Centwally.

Tim picked up speed, preparing to ram the group, but had to jam on the breaks when he noticed how many of them were in his way. Neither Craig, Armando, nor Tim could accurately count the number of creatures they were facing, but if forced, what looked like a couple hundred of Eve's drones were lined up two or three deep, heaving angrily at the truck.

# THIRTY
# SIX

**CRAIG, ONCE AGAIN, HAD TO** make a split-second decision. Most people don't understand that this is the only difference between a leader and a follower. Inspiring speeches were nice and all, but when the shit hits the fan, a leader can assess the situation, make a decision, and stick with it. Second-guessing yourself was pointless.

He looked at the monsters and then back into the cab of the truck. Armando was still holding his side from where he got stabbed and Tim looked at him nervously.

"I can't drive through all of them, Ike."

"I know. Listen. We need a distraction. When they move, you take off. Get Katy and Centwally at the water tower and get everyone back to the base. Do NOT come back for me, not this time. This isn't Afghanistan."

"Ike, if you step off this truck, you're dead," Armando said solemnly.

"If I don't, we're all dead. My mission, our mission was to get these civilians out of danger. They didn't say anything about me making it back."

"I want you to know, Ike. I never blamed you. You don't have to make some suicidal attempt at redemption. Everyone here forgives you," Tim said.

Craig felt the knot in his throat tighten a bit. He swallowed hard and earnestly said, "I don't forgive me. It's okay. Listen to Centwally, get Katy, and go live your lives. You all deserve it."

With that, Craig leaped off of the truck. He massaged his wound for a brief moment in order to get the blood flowing. Once he had a pool of it in the palm of his hand, he tossed the blood at the monstrosities. The smell of copper in the air moved the focus of the creatures from the truck to Craig.

"You did it now, stupid," Craig said to himself as he turned and began to run.

He did not need to turn around to hear the sounds of hundreds of pairs of feet chasing him. Over the chaos, he could hear the HDTT moving forward, completely unimpeded. Craig continued to run as fast as he could back toward the center of town. He wasn't sure where he was running to, but there was no way in hell he was stopping. The creatures chasing him were not going to stop. In fact, they had begun to gain ground on him. He could feel their hot breath on his neck with the smell of rotting meat getting stronger each time one of the monsters opened their mouth. It was when Craig felt a fingernail slide down his back that he put his motor into fifth gear.

Craig cut down the alley on Fifth and Main, his ability to turn easier than the monsters chasing him put a few more feet of distance between them. Craig hit the fence at the end of the alley, climbed the chicken wire, and flipped himself over to the other side. Landing on his feet, he turned to see the monsters run into the chicken wire, but they made no attempt to climb it. They just stood there, snarling at him and hissing but they did not make a move to jump, climb, or tear down the fence. It was at this moment that Craig started to think back to Afghanistan. Running through an alley into a hut, ducking and covering only for it all to lead him straight to where the enemy wanted him to go. It was happening again. He was allowing himself to run straight into an ambush. Craig turned again and began to run as fast as he could. This time, however, he had purpose. He made it out of the alley and onto Parker Street, according to the sign. He remembered from his briefing that Parker ran into another large farm. He could connect to the highway from there and possibly walk back to the base before the bomb dropped.

Having any plan was good enough for him at this point, even if it was paper-thin. He paused a moment to catch his breath when he heard the chicken wire a few dozen yards behind him snap. The sound of bodies falling to the ground was overtaken by the shrieks of delight from the creatures. Craig turned and began to run when he hit something that felt like a brick wall. He hit the ground with a hard thud. Dazed, he shook the cobwebs out of his head and looked up to see what he had run into. Standing above him was Eve.

# THIRTY
# SEVEN

**AFTER HE MUTTERED A FEW** curse words to himself, Craig lifted up his right leg and smashed the sole of his boot into Eve's shin. She looked down, unimpressed, reached out with both of her arms, and picked Craig off of the ground by his ears. Legs shaking in midair, Craig looked like a little kid. She bared her teeth at him, a sign of strength and intimidation in most animals. Rather than the four fangs, Eve displayed multiple rows of sharp, jagged, and orange-stained teeth. Craig wanted to close his eyes but was captivated by the chunks of raw meat and the stringy sinew hanging from her mouth. The smell was identical to a dead body starting to decompose. He thought he was going to pass out, but his fear of Eve had spiked his adrenaline to a new level. She sniffed all around his face and licked the sweat and dried blood covering his face. Her breath smelled of still rotting flesh and hot, thick blood. Craig finally found the courage to look her in the eyes; *if I'm dying, it will not be a coward*, he told himself.

Her face was stark white, mainly from the dry, flaky skin falling off of her every second, exposing greenish-yellow pustules hiding underneath the surface. Her nose resembled a pig's snout more than a human nose, and when her long, stringy, black hair kept falling in front of her jet-black eyes, they twitched white, as if she was blinking. Craig finally had to relent; *this bitch was definitely an alien*.

Eve dropped him back to the ground with a hard thud. He apparently wasn't worth her time. It was only after he was able to catch his breath that he realized all of her drones had surrounded him. They were all snarling and hissing at him but not attacking. Craig saw no way around it; he was as good as lunch meat at this point. Not the type to lay down and die, he slowly removed his knife one last time from the sheath on his belt.

Sentimentality was not his strong suit, but he found himself suddenly reliving all of the important moments in his life. His parents, Arlen and Cathy, who had shown him unconditional love—even when he didn't deserve it. Losing his virginity to Jill Simmons his freshman year. The first and only person he had ever loved, Tiffany. Boot camp, the comradery, finding his team, the brothers, being shot, betraying his friends—all of it came back to him in a flood. He nodded his head, thinking fondly of the good and the bad. He was at peace with whatever happened next.

With a previously unknown speed and strength, Craig thrust his knife into the side of Eve's kneecap. Once in, he ripped it out and thrust again at the same spot. Black ooze spurted out of her wound every time Craig pulled the knife out. He was six clean stabs into her knee, touching bone for the first time, when he was violently lifted off of his feet, his knife still stuck inside. Eve's drones all shouted out in glee as she held Craig high above her head by his left arm and leg. His wound, exposed and bleeding profusely, was too appetizing for Eve to resist. A hungry growl filled the air right before she buried her thirty-two teeth deep into Craig's ribs.

Craig cried out in a pure pain he had never felt before. All of the happy memories he had held so dear and true a few seconds ago were completely drained from his mind, along with the unlucky platelets of blood flowing past his rib cage. Just as Craig was certain he couldn't take anymore, Eve raised her blood-covered face from her meal and let out a shriek that would make a banshee run and hide. She let go of Craig's arm and left him dangling upside down, still holding onto his left leg. She lifted him slightly like he was a trophy and shrieked once again in the pouring rain. Eve began to convulse, slowly at first, like she was trying to suppress a cough. Still holding on to Craig, she could no longer hold it in and started to spew the black liquid that ran through her veins all over her soldiers. She was choking and gagging as if something were stuck in her esophagus.

Eve hissed at Craig and lifted him, upside down, to her eye level. She started to bring him closer to her mouth like she was going to take another bite when her body began to violently shake. Her mouth was open, and her eyes were wide with fear. He wasn't sure what exactly was happening, but he was positive he didn't want to be in her grasp when whatever this was had finished. Craig, unfortunately, got exactly what he wanted as Eve, still in the middle of a seizure, flung him like a rag doll.

Landing ten feet away from her gathering soldiers, he felt the ribs on the right side of his body crack when he landed. The pain of six ribs breaking simultaneously damn near made him pass out, but a voice in his head kept shouting at him to get up. He rolled himself over onto his back and tried to breathe but could not find any room in his chest to do so.

"Are you okay, Mr. Soldier?" Craig heard a voice ask.

He opened his eyes and saw a soft-eyed, large man standing over him. Craig held his hand out, and the man grabbed it and violently pulled Craig off of the ground. He could hear the sounds of feet running toward them. He didn't know what was happening, as if he were having some sort of dream, but he could have sworn someone was trying to help him. Someone was trying to save him. Craig managed to focus and start walking but was unable to actually move. The rain falling on his head felt like rocks hitting him, and his breathing was becoming few and far between. He wondered how much time he had left.

The sound of the feet running toward him grew louder, and he looked up to see a dozen or so of the creatures running straight at him. Seeing his imminent death running at him was actually a relief at this point. He was fucked up, and he knew it. His death was only a matter of time at this point, and he'd much rather be eaten by those things than suffocate on Parker Street in Helm's Hamlet, Iowa.

The creatures were six feet away from him and were beginning to show their teeth when the loudest noise, in the form of a scream, Craig had ever heard forced him to cover his ears. It turns out he had not imagined someone trying to help him as a man fell down next to him, also holding his ears in pain.

As quickly as it started, the sound stopped, and so did Eve's soldiers. They had stopped moving, stopped snarling and hissing. They just stood straight up and stared straight ahead. The man next to him stood up first and offered his hand for Craig to take. Craig did so and begged the guy to take it easy when lifting him up.

"Thank you," Craig muttered, trying to maintain some sort of rhythm in his breathing.

"Oh, wow! You sure is welcome, Mr. Soldier. I'm Byron, Byron Potts."

"Nice to meet you, Byron. I'm Craig Eitel," he said as he lost the ability to stay conscious and closed his eyes.

# THIRTY

# EIGHT

## BURN AFTER READING

**THE BRIGHT LIGHTS HE HAD** always been told about were brighter than he expected. He tried to focus on it, but the light was truly blinding. Instinct forced him to turn his head away, easing the pain in his eyes. It was then that he realized he was not dead. He continued to look around and saw the machines monitoring his heart rate, the IV drip running to his arm, and then felt the pain. He definitely was not in heaven. He was in the hospital. Craig hoped, at the very least, that Helm's Hamlet had been a horrible dream. Maybe he had gotten his ass kicked by Jimmy Spaski and ended up here. Those desperate thoughts were dashed when he recognized the woman sitting next to his bed.

"Agent Alexander?"

"Well, I think you can call me Ronda now, Craig."

"What happened?"

"That's why I'm here. I need to debrief you, but I can tell you're not quite ready for that. Rest up, soldier. You have a lot of work ahead of you."

Craig assumed she was talking about physical therapy but had a sneaking suspicion he was being incredibly naive. He wanted to protest, thinking he would just rather get the debrief over with, but his body told him differently. He winced and grunted in pain before Ronda showed him where the button was to administer his pain medication.

A week later, Craig was on his feet and out of the hospital. He had six broken ribs on his right side. His left side was blessed with over two hundred stitches from the multiple wounds he took at the Battle of Helm's Hamlet, but only one of his ribs had been kind enough to puncture a lung. If it wasn't for Byron, he would have died. He still, however, was unsure how the pair got out of that particular level of hell. He remembered very little but not enough. He was anxious to find out at today's meeting.

The team, Ronda, and Katy were set to meet at a vacant business center in downtown Des Moines, Iowa. Everyone had already arrived when Craig's cab pulled up in front of the building. He sat in the car for a minute. A week ago, his entire life was different. He was fighting local hoodlums as a mall security guard. Today, he was being debriefed over a mission where he fought vicious monsters, probably from another planet. The team he had betrayed eighteen months earlier, fighting beside him and they had won. No casualties. *What a difference a week can make,* he thought to himself.

"Hey, buddy. You in the wrong spot?" The cab driver asked, waking Craig from his daydream.

"Sorry, pal. What do I owe you?"

"That'll be $23.10, please."

Craig gave the cab driver a twenty and a ten, told him to keep the change, and then gingerly exited the back seat of the cab. He looked at the rundown, brown brick building and its blacked-out windows. A thought began to fester in the back of his mind; *this would be the perfect place to kill me.*

His goal, his long-term goal, had been to redeem himself after losing his honor by selling out his men. In his mind, he had achieved that goal. He was content. If Ronda and the agency felt it was time to dispose of Craig, he was fine with it. He would never just let them kill his boys, though. He was, however, happy to accommodate them if they wanted a fight. With a renewed sense of purpose, Craig held his head high and stepped through the glass doors of the office building.

The musty smell told Craig that this place had been vacant for a very long time. Ronda told Craig, upon meeting him at the front doors, that this was a black site and in everyone's best interests to keep this place looking as dilapidated as possible. The good news was that Ronda was talking to him. If they were going to wipe him out, it would have been done immediately. The mafia and intelligence world had that much in common.

The duo walked through the empty lobby to a set of elevators, neither saying a word. Inside the elevator, Ronda punched the button for the third floor and asked how Craig's ride over was. The pair shared more idle small talk while the elevator rose and light piano chords played over the elevator's speakers. The doors opened to a nearly empty office. There were no doors, just an open floor plan. In the middle of the room sat seven chairs and a long conference table. The music playing in the elevator was silenced by the music playing on a small radio on the middle of the table. At one end of the table was a large TV and VCR set up on a two-shelf cart. It reminded Craig of high school when the teacher didn't give a shit that day and just showed the class a movie or documentary loosely based on the subject they were supposed to have been studying.

Lou, Armando, and Tim were all sitting down, laughing and sipping on coffee. Katy was standing, one foot on her chair, laughing and smiling as always. Centwally was standing next to the coffee maker adding more sugar than a normal human should be ingesting into a steaming cup of black coffee. When they noticed Craig, everyone hooted and hollered for a couple seconds.

"Alright, boys. It's Saturday, and I got plans in Washington D.C. tonight, so let's get this over with," Ronda said, walking with Craig to their seats.

"Didn't you have plans in Washington when we first met?" Craig asked as Katy reached across the table and turned the radio off.

"Yes, sweetheart. Momma always has plans on Saturday night."

The boys all whistled quietly while Lou and Centwally nodded their heads in approval.

The full debrief took a little over two hours. Each member detailed exactly what they did, what they saw, who or what they killed, and their return back to base safely with the survivors of Helm's Hamlet. They had met no resistance once they had loaded all of the women into the HDTT, Craig assuming he was lucky enough to have drawn the ire of the entire batch of creatures.

Craig, however, was not asked to speak next. Ronda stood up and removed a VHS tape from her bag resting on the table. She silently walked over to the TV and VCR set up, turned the TV on, and inserted the tape into the video player. After she picked up the remote control from on top of the VCR, she touched the play button on the remote and strode back to her seat.

The picture was fuzzy for a minute before the picture came to life. A large man was sitting in a chair at a steel table. He looked terrified. Craig looked around the table, and it was evident that he was the only person confused as to who this man was.

"It's ok, son," a voice said from the other side of the camera, "tell us your name."

"My name is B-B-Byron. Byron Potts."

"Hi, Byron. It sure is nice to meet you," the woman behind the camera said. Her voice was high-pitched, yet soft... like she was speaking to a baby.

The man continued, "Byron, can you look up at me."

Once Byron did as he was told, she started to speak again, "Byron, my name is Agent Katherine Rigol... but you can call me Katy. I'm so happy to meet you, Byron. Do you know why?"

"No..." Byron said, looking around the room for a clue.

"I'm happy to meet you because you are a hero, Byron."

It took a second or two for the words to sink in, but once he was able to comprehend that he was the hero, that she was talking to him, his entire demeanor changed.

"I'ms a hero," he asked, sitting upright in his chair for the first time.

"You sure are! Do you remember saving my friend?"

"I sures do, but I's was so scared. Aaron says real mens are never ever scared of nothin'."

"Was Aaron your friend?"

Byron's attitude shifted again as he slouched in his chair and his chin began to quiver.

Katy prodded him again, "Byron, where is Aaron?"

"Hims gots real mad at me. Hims said I was the 'r word' and then run offs when we was ats his gubnerment offices."

Ronda paused the tape and glanced around the room. The scowl on her face did not waiver as she began to speak.

"You let the leader of these sex trafficking, white nationalist shitheads get away? Should I be thanking Eve if we find him amongst the goo and guts left in that ghost town?"

The question was clearly rhetorical, but just in case it was unclear to anyone around the table, Ronda hit the play button on the remote control again.

"I am very sorry he said those things to you, Byron. I think he's a dumb ass," Katy said on the tape.

Byron giggled and looked up again, a shy grin on his face like he wasn't supposed to be laughing and was trying not to get caught.

"What happened after Aaron ran away?"

Byron shifted a bit in his seat, scratched the top of his head, and said, "I's hid on the roof. Nobodies goes up on the roof... I'm not allowed, but I's is the bestest spy in Iowa."

"I bet you are," Katy said, "What did you see on the roof?"

"I's seent the soldier man running and running. Hims the fastest soldier I's ever seent... but he runs into the big lady."

"Did you hide when the soldier man got caught?"

Byron looked almost insulted, "No ways. I's is the most bravest spy in Iowa. I's saw everything. I's even saw her tries to eat the soldier mans."

Katy pressed a bit harder, her voice switching back to her regular speaking voice. She was starting to get to the information she was really interrogating Byron for and knew this was the time to sound more like a mother than a friend. She needed him to remember and articulate everything he saw, as Byron Potts was the only eyewitness to what killed Eve.

"Now, Byron, I need you to think very hard here. What happened when the 'big lady' tried to eat the 'soldier man'?"

"Oh, hers did not liked the ways he tasted..."

Ronda had to pause the tape again. This time it was due to the laughter ripping through the room, as contagious as a yawn. Even Ronda broke and started to chuckle. After a few seconds, she silenced the boys by clearing her throat and sitting up straight again in her seat. Everyone around the table followed her lead, adjusted their posture, and once silent, Ronda hit play for the last time on the remote control.

"...the big lady started to choke. Aaron tolds me I's was all-jerk-ic to strawberries. I's eat one this one times, and I's chokeded too."

"Oh no! We better not give you any of those for breakfast, huh," Katy asked with a chuckle.

Byron giggled too, but as soon as Katy asked him to continue his story, he explained that once he had seen Eve choking, he started to run away because he was scared. It was only when he had climbed down from the roof and began to run that he saw Craig thrown by Eve. Byron wanted another friend and thought that Craig would basically be his new Aaron. The thought of this gave Craig a chill. Being associated with that supremacist piece of shit was repulsive but had it not been for Byron, Craig would be dead.

Byron wrapped up his story on the videotape by explaining how Eve's soldiers had froze the second she died.

"Thank you, Byron. You did a great job, you big ol' hero you," Katy said.

Byron's massive smile is where the tape stopped.

Ronda stood again and turned the TV off by unplugging the electronics from the plug built into the cart. She turned to face the group gathered around the table.

"So, do we have any theories?"

"Theories?" Craig asked, not understanding the question.

"What killed Eve?"

Craig looked around the table and decided he would be the bad guy.

"Had you not dropped a MOAB on the town, we may be able to study her. Take DNA samples."

Ronda sighed her signature sigh and explained, "No bombs were dropped on Helm's Hamlet."

"None?"

"Not a single one. Armando, any guesses," Ronda asked, looking directly at the team's medic.

"Umm... well, Byron said something about being allergic. Are women of all kinds allergic to Craig?"

"Correct, all women are allergic to Craig, but also... that's not quite what did the job. According to Armando's report, he administered an excessive amount of the blood clotting powder he keeps in his kit on your wound."

"Affirmative," Armando said.

"Her system couldn't handle the amount of coagulated blood she ingested. Based on everything we now know, her reaction to that powder on Craig's wound was similar to one of us ingesting arsenic."

"Why didn't the soldiers attack Craig or Byron, though?" Tim asked, forever thankful Bonnie stopped him from killing Byron in the bank vault.

"Best we can tell is that when she died, they lost brain function. We had teams monitor the situation until dawn. They didn't move an inch the rest of the night, even when the sun rose and burnt them to ash," Ronda concluded.

The team got up, most of them talking about what strip club to have breakfast at, when Ronda reminded everyone that they were not yet dismissed. Confused, everyone sat back down and waited for her to clue them in.

"Now, we discussed earlier that you would be free men if you completed your mission. Well, you completed your mission. As a lady of my word, I have your pardons right here. All signed and ready for you or your attorneys to review. I beg you, though, please, no lawyers. None of them have the clearance to understand the deal you're about to make. While it would be fun to kill a few, I don't have the time."

Each man took the paper and began to read it over. Craig studied the body language of everyone as they read. Everyone seemed to be excited. That is until they got to paragraph three.

"What the fuck does conditional release mean?" Lou asked.

Everyone turned toward Ronda as that was the question they had as well.

"It means you're pardoned *if.*"

"*If* what? Don't you remember I took some hillbilly's dirty knife to the gut?" Armando asked, getting annoyed.

"No, you don't need to remind me because it was your ribs, not your gut. Quit whining. Conditional means you are released on one condition."

"And what condition is that, ma'am?" Lou asked.

"You work for me. You are my team. Craig stays in place as your lead. Katy is your newest member, replacing Paul. Deal?"

The guys looked at Craig, who nodded his head in agreement. Lou was the first to sign, followed by Centwally, then Armando, then Tim. Craig, being genuinely excited, shot up and clapped like he had just won the big game. The pain was intense, but he didn't care.

Ronda looked around the room and nodded with a smirk. She looked at Craig, who sat down a bit sheepishly.

"Now that that is all settled and done. We've got a nasty son of a bitch that just took over a small Central American country through a brutal military coup. Who's ready to go to work?"

Craig smiled as the team sat up straight and began to study the files Katy was handing out. For the first time in almost two years, Craig had his family back. At the end of the day, that is all that really mattered.

THE END

*Thank you for reading!*

*Go to 5310PUBLISHING.COM*
*for more great books you can read today!*

*If you enjoyed this book, please review it!*

Connect with us on social media!
@5310publishing on Twitter and Instagram

Subscribe to our mailing list to get exclusive
offers, news, updates, and discounts for our
future book releases and our authors!

# You might also like...
## *HONEY BEAUMONT*

Once upon a time, an unlikely hero was born out of servitude. Honey Beaumont, our hero, strived to do right by everyone and see justice prevail no matter the consequence. He dreamt of the intrepid Adventurer's Guild and helping those who can't help themselves.

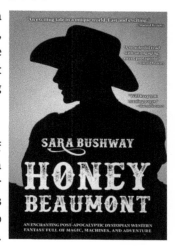

Every day Honey persevered the wrath of Byron, his owner. Helping those around him doesn't fill Byron's pockets, bringing out anger in his boss. One day, Byron brutally attacks Honey after a wealthy client offers to help Honey leave the life of servitude and be free. After the attack, Honey was scarred, disfigured, and with a grudge. He begrudgingly left his home and the love of his life behind to move into a new and luxurious home.

Honey mingles amongst those in the new house and learns about the world's inequalities, especially between the nobodies and humans. But with his new owner forbidding him from being independent, Honey has no other choice but to leave this new luxurious life behind.

Freedom for Honey meant joining the Adventure's Guild, becoming a hero, and helping his family leave the horrible place he used to call home. Will Honey be strong enough to take on Byron? Only time will tell.

Embarking on a journey of a lifetime, being a hero is harder than Honey ever imagined, but at least he has his friends by his side to help him save the day.

SCAN ME

# You might also like...
## MAGIC OF LIES

Princess Eirian Altira has always walked on a knife's edge with flowers chasing her footsteps. Born with magic, she struggles to balance her ability to give life with the desire to kill. Raised by mages, the day comes when she must return home to a kingdom she left as a child, and a father she has not seen in 20 years. Surrounded by a strange court with expectations she was not prepared for, Eirian hides her magic until she's faced with the choice between becoming queen or returning to the mages.

With secrets around every corner and war with a neighboring kingdom on the horizon, Eirian discovers her power means more than she realized. As does her long-standing friendship with the crown prince of the elven nation they've been allied with for generations. But the whispers in her mind and the rumors spreading through her court threaten everything Eirian holds dear, and she will do anything to protect the ones she loves.

----------

*"You don't know what I'm capable of or what I'm willing to do. Don't underestimate me. You might regret it."*

----------

When Eirian Altira returned home after decades away, she thought it would be a fresh start. Raised a mage in a distant city, she struggles to adjust to life as a princess in a court where magic is undesired. Caught between two thrones, she knows where her duty lies. With assassination attempts and rumors of war, Eirian proves to those around her that she is not one to hide from confrontation. Even when it risks her life.

Torn between her love for a man sent far from her side, her attraction to the captain of her guards, and the best friend she has always needed, Eirian refuses to bow to the demands of her advisors. Determined to be the queen

her kingdom needs her to be in the face of war, Eirian seeks the truth behind who she is and why the enigmatic land they have never had dealings with is seeking an alliance. But the answer may not be what she expected, and the repercussions could cost her the very throne she must defend.

SCAN ME

Lightning Source UK Ltd.
Milton Keynes UK
UKHW011958280223
417834UK00004B/10